LAST RITES

"Where are you hurt my friend?"

"As deep as the knife could reach." The man tried to raise his head. His breathing was easier. "Who are you?"

"A friend. I'm a priest."

"Who, not what." The man rested his head on the back of his hand, the long fingers spread and glistening with spittle.

"Joseph McMahon," the priest said. "Shall I go for a doctor if you don't want a priest?"

"It's as late for one as the other, wouldn't you say?"

DOROTHY SALISBURY DAVIS

"SHE BELONGS IN THE SAME COMPANY AS DASHIELL HAMMETT, RAYMOND CHANDLER AND JOSEPHINE TEY."
Denver Post

Other Avon Books by
Dorothy Salisbury Davis

TALES FOR A STORMY NIGHT

Coming Soon

THE PALE BETRAYER

WHERE THE DARK STREETS GO

DOROTHY SALISBURY DAVIS

 AVON
PUBLISHERS OF BARD, CAMELOT, DISCUS AND FLARE BOOKS

AVON BOOKS
A division of
The Hearst Corporation
1790 Broadway
New York, New York 10019

Copyright © 1969 by Dorothy Salisbury Davis
Published by arrangement with the author
Library of Congress Catalog Card Number: 71-85261
ISBN: 0-380-70131-6

First Avon Printing: September 1986

Printed in the U.S.A.

K–R   10 9 8 7 6 5 4 3 2 1

WHERE THE DARK STREETS GO

1

Father McMahon was leaning out the window of the rectory study when he saw the boy in the distance. A little fellow, he was running with all his might in a crazy zigzag fashion, dodging cars and ashcans, a pile of junk and a cluster of women. When he came closer the priest recognized him, and at the moment he recognized him he realized he had found his way into Sunday's sermon: brotherhood was a matter of getting close enough to recognize one another. Since for over an hour he had been at the desk sorting banalities like a curate his shoes to see which pair was the least run down, he sat on the window ledge, swung his legs out and dropped to the sidewalk below. It was spring and the slow rain of early morning had left the smell of earth behind it, earth and the river smell which told of the tide's turning and provoked his memory of the sea's edge and the sand's whiteness, and himself the stranger running there in what once he had thought of as self-pursuit. Always he identified with runners.

He braced himself and spread his arms. "Hold it, Carlos. Slow down."

The youngster crashed into him. When the priest had steadied him on his feet the boy caught his hand and pulled at him. "Come, Father, quick. My friend, the man, he is hurt very bad."

"You can tell me on the way." The priest set his pace by the boy's, his long stride one to the boy's three steps. "Did he send for a priest?"

"No, Father, *si*." Carlos often mixed yes and no as well

as his languages. He was growing up bilingual in New York, or, as the monsignors said dryly of the rapidly increasing minority among his parishioners, semilingual.

"Are the police there, Carlos?" he asked as they approached Tenth Avenue.

"No, Father. Nobody."

That, the priest thought, would be strange indeed in the crowded tenement where Carlos lived. But the boy led the way, racing against a change in the traffic light and the bursting surge of trucks and taxis. Down a block he ran, then west again to a building marked for demolition, the great white X's scarring the windows. The whole long street, beyond and on both sides, was a desolation. The bulldozers had leveled the rubble to a prairie flatness. The boy led him down three steps and through a basement entry. How he had come to know the man was there, God only knew. The passageway was dank, bile-green, and piled with molding rubbish.

Carlos stopped at a half-open door. "In there, Father."

The priest heard the man's breathing before he saw him, the rattling sound of it all too familiar. The man lay, face down, on a heap of old clothes and bedding. The broken window overhead fronted on the street. McMahon glimpsed the top of a passing truck. He looked around for the boy to instruct him, but Carlos had vanished. He called out his name.

His own voice came faintly back, and then, as he approached the man and knelt beside him, he heard the child pass beneath the window. "Bring your mother, Carlos!" he called to him.

"If you can find your mother, Carlos," the man said with a clarity the priest had not expected.

"Where are you hurt, my friend?"

"As deep as the knife could reach." The man tried to raise his head. His breathing was easier. "Who are you?"

"A friend. I'm a priest."

"Who? Not what." The man rested his head on the back of his hand, the long fingers spread and glistening with spittle. In the gray light his gray face with its glaring eyes and dark beard resembled a medieval Christus.

"Joseph McMahon," the priest said. "Shall I go for a doctor if you don't want a priest?"

"It's as late for one as the other, wouldn't you say?"

"You are alive, man. It's not that late."

"Ah-h-h . . ." The sound trailed off. He tried to clear his throat of the rasp starting there again. "You've heard the noise of death in your business."

"Too many times," the priest said.

"I can't get it out of my throat. Come down where I can see you. Turn your face to the light." He lifted his free hand and let it fall in the patch of daylight out of which he then dragged it like something separately alive, a haunting hand, the priest thought, the long fingers squared at the tips. The man clutched it in against himself.

McMahon lay down on the cold cement, flat on his stomach, his face toward the window within a foot or so of the dying man's. He could smell the taint of death. The whites of the man's eyes shone as he tried to focus them on the priest's face. "I think I would like to know you, Joseph McMahon."

"Tell me what I can do to help you."

"Get rid of the pain. Can you do that?"

"I would if I could, God knows."

"Then talk to me. Talk to me of anything but death. What were you doing when the child came for you?"

It was like tunneling out of a dream, going back that little time ago when he had been sitting at the study desk. "I was trying to write a sermon."

"Oh, God almighty. I'm glad I got you away from that."

McMahon laughed. He could not help it, and he was glad, for he saw that it pleased the man. "I would like to know you too, my friend."

"Is it so?"

"It is so."

The eyes slid away from the priest's face, staring past him. When he tried to speak the bloody spittle bubbled up to his lips. McMahon wiped it away with his own hand-kerchief. The man said, "Nim said once I'd shake hands with the devil."

"Is that what I am to you?"

"No, no, I was only remembering. Do you believe in him, horns, tail and all?"

"I believe in evil, call it what you will."

"So do I, friend. Oh, yes. So do I."

"Do you want to tell me what happened to you?" the priest asked gently.

"No. And I don't want you telling me what is going to happen to me."

"I wouldn't presume to."

"Forgive me, but you are a priest. Do you believe what you wrote in that sermon?"

"I try to write what I believe."

"Are you sure it's not the other way around?"

McMahon had the feeling of dream again, the self-aware dream where you know you are dreaming and so let things go that you might otherwise hold back. "No. I am not sure."

The man showed his teeth in a smile that became a grimace. He burrowed his face in his arm. His whole body shivered with every tearing breath. McMahon stroked the back of his head. He could think of no other comfort to offer, and he could not fortify even himself with prayer.

"You ought to tell me," he tried again.

The man turned his head. "Why? So you could save his soul?"

"Just to take the knife away from him."

"I think I've taken the knife . . ." He cradled his head again in the crook of his arm, the face buried. The shoulders grew still, the breathing stopped.

McMahon heard the scraping of his own shoes as he got to his knees. He knelt on, looking down at the remnant of mortality, an existence no longer, a man who had, the instant before, left off being himself to himself, being. Into your hands, O Lord, I commend his spirit. He commends his spirit. The priest lingered still and listened to the deep silence of the cellar, the deeper seeming because of the far noises of the city, the *ack-ack* of a pneumatic drill, the thump of the demolition sledge, the deep-throated horn of a docking liner. He got to his feet and went out.

The sunlight was a shock to his eyes. He looked down. The words "Love Power" were scrawled on the sidewalk.

At the first call box on Tenth Avenue he telephoned the police. Then, because he was so instructed, he started back toward the building to await their arrival. He found himself almost greedily aware of life on that little journey: oranges in a basket were like so many suns. He picked one up and turned it in his hand. The shopkeeper rushed out and urged him to have it. He shook his head and put it back carefully. Most people knew him, the women in doorways haloed in hair curlers sunning themselves and their infants, store-keepers and cart vendors, the walkers of dogs, even the dogs. They all knew a priest for a priest if not for a man. A strange thought that, wherever it came from. Then he remembered: *Who? Not what.*

He asked among the women on the stoop of the walkup where Carlos lived if any of them had seen the boy. No one had.

"What did he do, Father?" Their eagerness to hear of mischief was implicit.

"Nothing, nothing. He is a good boy."

"Si, they are all good boys," an old one said, wagging her head.

"His mother, she is not home so much," another offered, trying to detain him with the suggestion of gossip.

McMahon walked on. *If you can find your mother, Carlos:* did that mean the dead man knew her? The police would gather and sift the gossip and shake out bits of truth. He heard the first siren as he turned the corner. Waiting, staring at the rubbled field, he caught sight of two doors leaned together like a tent with a tiny flag hoisted atop one end. That would be the first place to look for Carlos.

* * *

Detective Finley Brogan took McMahon's statement while they sat in the back of a squad car outside the building. The whole area was being cordoned off, for the crowd came quickly at the siren's wail. Technical trucks, a mobile generator, an ambulance, and car after car of police and detectives converged. Nor were they all investigative. Any incident could fuse the neighborhood, a mixture of blacks and whites, Puerto Rican, Italian and Irish. Volatile, combustible.

Brogan was a well-mannered young detective brought up with a proper respect for the clergy. He asked every question as though it might encroach on the privacy of the confessional. Not so Lieutenant Traynor. When he climbed into the car with them Brogan proposed to read him the priest's statement.

Traynor said, "I don't think it would tire Father McMahon to go over it again. Would it, Father?" His smile was quick to come and go, a weapon of sorts. He was a man of around McMahon's age, forty, lean and scrubbed-looking, with slate-gray eyes. The name was an old one in the parish records.

When McMahon had told the story again, Traynor asked: "Did he come for you, or would any priest have done?"

"Any priest. I happened to be the one at hand." It crossed his mind that the dialogue between the dying man and either of the other two curates would have been quite different. To say nothing of how the monsignor would have dealt with the situation.

"You've never seen him around the neighborhood?"

"Not to my knowledge, but he would have looked different under other circumstances."

"A beard is a beard," Traynor said.

"I got the impression the boy knew him."

"What other impression did you get, Father?"

McMahon hesitated. They were numerous, but he would have to sort them out, to think about them.

"Did he know his killer, for example?"

"He might have."

"Did you ask him?"

"It's there in the notes," McMahon said, pointing to the report book in Brogan's hands. "I asked him if he wanted to tell me what happened to him."

"You were real delicate with him, Father. Because he wasn't a Catholic?"

McMahon felt the prickle of temper. "I'd have been as delicate with a Catholic."

"And him on the point of death?"

Both the questions and answers were wrong, almost the reverse, McMahon thought, of what either of them wanted to say.

"He did not want my advice," he said, trying to end the matter.

Traynor grunted. "There's a girl's name in there some place. No message for her?"

"Lieutenant, I have told as closely as I remember what was said. He gave me no sense of urgency on his behalf, no message, no regret, none of the things we feel should concern a man who knows he is about to die."

"Then why do you suppose he sent the child for you?"

"I'm not sure he did. It may have been Carlos' own idea."

"Then what was the kid doing there?"

"We'll have to ask him that."

Traynor thought about it, his eyes meanwhile sharp to the coming and going of his men. An unmarked car sirened its way alongside them. "The glamour boys," Tranor grumbled, and opened the door to get out. It was only later that McMahon learned he meant the Homicide Division. To Brogan he said: "Pick the youngster up," and then to McMahon: "Puerto Rican?"

"Yes."

"Black or white?"

"White." McMahon did not say it, but Carlos' sisters looked Negroid.

"I grew up in this neighborhood," Traynor said. "But it

was a different place then. St. Peter's church. Is that your parish, Father?"

"Yes."

"Give my respects to Monsignor Casey. Does the kid speak English?"

"He can manage pretty well when he tries," the priest said.

"Most of them can. That's the whole problem, isn't it?"

McMahon did not think so but he refrained from saying it. Traynor shook hands with the men Brogan then identified to the priest as Homicide. He and McMahon got out the other side of the car.

"I could use your help with the youngster, Father."

To avoid the following eyes of the curious, McMahon walked the detective to Tenth Avenue. He pointed out the building where Carlos lived, the stoop now deserted. The detective made a note of the address. "It's only a hunch where we're going," the priest said, "but we'll find him one place or another."

"Do you speak Spanish, Father?"

"Well, I don't suppose a Spaniard would call it that."

Brogan grinned. "I'd have the same trouble with an Englishman."

"You don't live in the parish, do you, Brogan?"

"No, Father. In Chelsea, what's left of that. My old man is a longshoreman. Same as Traynor's, only his father's a big *macher* in the union."

"A good English word," McMahon said.

The boy did not come out of his shelter until McMahon leaned down and drew aside the canvas flap which had been tacked on the dirty green doors. The canvas itself was smeared with paint. No child of Carlos' age could have put the play fort together. He came out on all fours when he saw it was the priest.

"This is a friend of mine, Detective Brogan. Carlos Morales."

Brogan stuck out his hand but the child did not take it.

Brogan admired the fort, but still won no favor. The boy looked only at the ground.

"Did your friend build it for you?" McMahon asked.

"*Si*, Father. Him and my brother."

"Are they friends?"

"*Si*."

Brogan reached for his report book and then thought the better of it.

"When did they build it?"

"For my saint's day."

"What's your friend's name?"

The boy shrugged.

"What do you call him?"

"*Amigo*."

McMahon and Brogan exchanged glances. The detective shrugged.

"Do you know where he lives?" the priest asked.

"In my house."

McMahon put the next question as carefully as he could. "Did you often visit him in the place you took me this morning?"

"Never." Finally the boy looked up at him. "I just go to the steps and call him. He comes down and gives me doorknobs. Would you like to see, Father?"

"I would."

While the boy went into the shelter, Brogan said, "You're doing fine, Father. We'll put it together afterwards."

Carlos hauled out a dogfood carton in which were a dozen or so doorknobs that had once been white but were now painted, some with faces, some like psychedelic Easter eggs.

"Oh, man," McMahon said, "aren't they something."

"Beautiful," Brogan said.

The boy grinned. "Every day when I come from school, he gives me one. If I say what I learned in school."

"Carlos only goes to school in the morning," McMahon explained to Brogan, which in no way explained why he was not in school that morning.

"This week I start afternoons, Father."

"So you went early to see your friend?"

Brogan shook his head. He did not like the prompting.

The boy said, "Yes, Father. Only he did not come when I call. I call again. Then he call me. 'I am hurt, Carlos,' and he tell me to come in the basement. I want to run away, but he say, 'Please, Carlos.' So I go in. He was like this." The boy humped over, hugging his hands to his chest. "He say, 'Don't be afraid,' but I am afraid when I see the blood. And when he fall down and don't talk any more I come for you."

"Carlos, do you remember the first time you ever saw the man, the first time?"

"*Si,* Father. He was painting Mrs. Phelan's door. He let me paint too."

Brogan asked his first question: "Did you see anyone else in the building where your friend was hurt?"

The boy glanced at the priest.

"Tell him," McMahon said.

"No."

"Not ever?"

The boy shook his head.

"You're a good boy, Carlos," the priest said. "Better put your doorknobs away now."

About to go into the hut, the boy saw the crowd for the first time. He looked up at the priest.

"I'll wait for you," McMahon said. Then to Brogan: "I'll have to tell him."

"Thanks a lot, Father. It may not sit with Traynor, but if you'll come round to the station this afternoon, we'll try it on him. Do you know this Mrs. Phelan he mentioned?"

"She owns the buildings I pointed out to you. She lives on the first floor." He knew Mrs. Phelan very well, but he was not going to say that to the detective.

"Is there a Mr. Phelan?"

"Yes," the priest said tersely.

"Okay, Father," Brogan said after waiting purposely for

the priest to go on. "I guess I can find out for myself what that's all about."

McMahon watched the detective take a short cut across the field. "Come, Carlos," he said. "I'll walk you home."

2

"Joseph? Father McMahon, you're late for luncheon."

He had hoped to get by the dining-room door without being seen, but the old man was watching for him. He sat like a family scion at the head of his table, and although there were only the two of them present, Father Purdy, the youngest priest of the four attached to the parish, sat in his own place, two chairs down, on the monsignor's left.

"I'll be right in," McMahon said. "I have to clean up a bit."

Miss Lalor, the housekeeper, poked her head out of the kitchen. "Will I set your soup, Father?"

"Not till he's at the table," the monsignor answered for him. "There's nothing worse than a slop of cold soup."

"He'll be in a hurry, Monsignor."

McMahon left them to settle the service of his lunch between them. They had been bickering for over twenty years. Monsignor Casey had brought her from Ireland after the war. That too was a matter on which they contended: whether she should have come or stayed in Galway and married a man with a mule and a garden. She was, by Father McMahon's lights, one of those women destined from the cradle to become a caretaker of priests. She was also one of the best cooks in the archdiocese—the hallway was sweet with the fragrance of her Friday pudding—but since St. Peter's was becoming more and more a poor parish, it was the monsignor's tart pleasure to end most of their arguments by saying it was time he gave her over to someone who could keep her in the style to which she was accustomed.

Their relationship was something McMahon sometimes thought about: the naturalness of it, the unnatural made natural somewhere in Ireland generations ago.

Whatever stain it was he had picked up on the basement floor was not going to come out of his clothes with spot remover. He had to change into his other suit. Paint or tar or blood. He sniffed at it: the smell was not strong enough to overcome Miss Lalor's sugar and spice. He was indeed late, he noticed by the clock on top of the piano. So he took another moment and gathered the music on which he had been working the night before, the score to Rachmaninoff's *The Bells*. He had arranged it himself for female voices. It was something the high-school girls could really swing on.

He ran down the steps and laid his briefcase on the hall table. He remembered then the half-written sermon he had left on the study desk and went to the front of the house to get it. *Do you believe what you wrote in that sermon?* I try to write what I believe. *Or is it the other way around?* A devil's advocate could not have attacked more succinctly. He wanted to think about that and about the dead man. Instead he sat down and made a note on brotherhood, the thought that had come into his mind when he recognized the running child. It no longer seemed very original.

Miss Lalor came to the study door. "Father, he's getting into a temper."

"I'm coming." He would as soon have gone without lunch and gained himself a few minutes for thought, but he followed her down the hall and paused only long enough to stuff the sermon into his briefcase.

"Was he a hippie, do you think?" The monsignor loved the word for some reason although he had little use for its designate.

"An old one then," McMahon said. "The police will soon know."

"They're the worst kind. It's a short step from the East Village to the Bowery."

"No, I don't think he was that kind."

"A pervert maybe?"

"What makes you say that?"

"The child, the child." The old man was as impatient with the cream jug, pouring the cream with a splash over his pudding.

"It was a healthy relationship, I'm sure."

"Healthy. Never mind was it healthy. Was it moral?"

"That's what I meant," McMahon said.

"Then why don't you say it? I can't stand these quibbling words you young fellows come up with nowadays."

McMahon ate in silence. Father Purdy folded his napkin and asked if he might be excused.

"We haven't upset you?" the monsignor said with an almost mocking tolerance he assumed toward the young priest. Purdy was earnest and easily put down. In his year among them he had not come to understand that the old man's brusqueness was his style and a carefully cultivated one. Purdy flushed when anything harsh or intimate was said in his presence and McMahon suspected that his show of naïveté was a style with him also. His own lack of patience with the boy priest, as he called him, was sometimes close to contempt.

"I have a Christian Doctrine class at one, Monsignor," Purdy said. Which, since the class was actually described as Ecumenism in the new curriculum, did not ingratiate him with McMahon, however the old-fashioned words might please the monsignor.

"Lieutenant Traynor asked to be remembered to you," McMahon said when Purdy had left the table.

"Is that Mike Traynor's son? A lieutenant? I thought he'd go up in a hurry, but not that much of a hurry." The old man sat back in his chair and dabbed his whole face with his napkin. His normally pink complexion always went florid by the end of the meal. "I baptized him . . . No, I suppose not. It's his confirmation I'm remembering. There was the question of the sponsor, one of the labor men his father wanted. I think he was a Communist. An ex-Communist, that was it." He laughed to himself then, remembering. "I can see Mike now, those shaggy brows of his going up."

He mimicked the brogue as though he had not a trace of one himself. "'Father Casey, half our executive are ex-Communists. It was the mixed marriage of the 'thirties.'"

Miss Lalor brought McMahon his pudding.

"Would you put it aside for me and I'll have it later, Miss Lalor. My singing girls will be waiting for me."

She returned to the kitchen, throwing a shoulder block on the swinging door.

Monsignor Casey said: "Is there a tune to it, whatever you're teaching them now, Joseph?"

"Oh, a lively tune, Monsignor," he said and blessed himself and left the table. The question was rote as was his answer, but he never failed to rankle under it, which he supposed was a lack of humility in himself. That the monsignor was proud of the St. Peter's Girls' Choir, he knew. It had some little fame in the archdiocese. The girls had sung for the Holy Father during his visit to New York and every year they gave several interfaith benefit concerts. McMahon was fairly sure that it was his work with them that forestalled his transfer to a larger parish or to one of his own, the latter an assignment he truly did not want.

He sat at the piano improvising softly while the girls filed in, the long and the short, the skinny and the squat, the black and the white, the knock-kneed, the piano-legged. Though they sang with the voices of angels, they came in like a herd of elephants. When Sister Justine had them in their places, he warmed them up with a few minutes of folk rock. He enjoyed the anachronism it made of him in their eyes. He was a stern disciplinarian and his tastes in music were as severe. Yet he loved to shake them loose this way, to set their breasts and buttocks bobbing, all of them letting go. Or almost all of them. Some of them were pretending. There was the sadness, the pretense. To please him? To fit in? It was a kind of self-denial, the kind he did not like, and he caught an image of these pretenders marching into their futures, into marriage, motherhood, or into maidenhood, treading the heels of these very shadows they were casting now before them. He realized that beneath the musings he was thinking of Priscella Phelan and the marriage he had been trying to mend although he deeply felt it should be dissolved.

He ended with a kind of *Eulenspiegel* fillip. The groans and laments were shut off by the staccato snaps of Sister Justine's frog. The snapper was as familiar to her fingers as the beads of her rosary. He got up from the piano and gave over the bench to sister who would play such notes as he needed to structure the *a cappella*.

"The Bells," he said, while the music was being passed. "We shall work only with sounds today. Forget the words. For most of you that won't be any hardship. All the sopranos: Bell, bell, bell. First altos, bong, bong, bong. Second altos, boom, boom, boom . . ."

Throughout the rehearsal his mind kept going back to the man in the cellar and to the child, Carlos, who took the word of his death as philosophically as the going away of someone he had known, his own father, for example. Carlos' sisters, Anita and Fran, were in the choir, and after practice McMahon detained them and spoke to the elder of the two.

"Did you go home to lunch today, Anita?"

"Yes, Father."

"Was Carlos there?" He had told the boy to remain at home until his sisters came. His mother was away at work.

"Yes, Father. There were policemen. They came looking for Pedrito. Everywhere they looked like he was hiding and they asked us questions."

"What questions?"

Anita looked to her sister for help, but Fran was shy. A homely, awkward girl, she never expected to be called upon, and he wished then that he had addressed her first.

"About where Pedrito worked. What time he went to work. My mother. And about Mr. Muller."

"Mr. Muller," McMahon repeated.

"He was killed with a knife. They asked did Pedrito have a knife. I would not tell them. Pedrito does not like the police. Nobody likes police in our house."

"Did you know Mr. Muller?"

"Yes, Father. He was a very nice man. He came to Carlos' saint's day."

"And he sings songs he makes up for Carlos, for my mother so she laugh, for everybody." This was Fran. Muller had obviously been able to draw even her out.

"You both liked him, did you?"

The girls nodded.

Anita said, "The police, they want to know who did not like him. And Mrs. Vargas tell them, Mr. Phelan. She don't like Mr. Phelan, you see, Father. Otherwise, she don't tell anything."

McMahon did not like gathering gossip from the girls. Nor did he want to make them late for their next class. "Did you take Carlos to school this afternoon?"

"Yes, Father. He don't want to go, but we made him go. Otherwise..." Anita gave herself an uninhibited slap on the rump by way of illustration.

3

McMahon finished his sermon when he got back to the rectory. He did not like it at all now: brotherhood and closeness, a sentimental myth. He found himself testing each phrase in the light of the dying man's challenge, and he wanted to cross out more of what he had written than he wanted to retain. He was annoyed with himself. Or with the dead man? See here, he wanted to say, perfection is a luxury. But faith is a greater luxury. Where the latter thought had come from he did not know. He had provided his antagonist with dialogue. Perfection should be a goal, and to a priest faith was a necessity. The only marks he put on the paper in the end were the dashes with which he always marked his breathing places, and while he tested these, his mind slipped comfortably off to the parish priest of his childhood, upstate, who seemed not to take a breath from the first word to the last of his sermon. At the breakfast table after the eight o'clock Mass when Father Dunne had preached, the family would piece together what it was he had said. McMahon could remember now his father's saying: "It may seem like a great joke, but stop and think about this: you'll remember years from now some of the things we've figured out here at the table, and some of the mission priests with their fire and brimstone you'll forget forever." And it was true: many a sermon he had himself built on a few words caught from Father Dunne's whirlwind.

Monsignor Casey came to the study door. "Mrs. Phelan is in the parlor asking to see you. She says it's important."

"She might have phoned first," McMahon said. His eyes went to the windows as though in search of escape.

"Let me talk to her then. I'm an old man with some of my troubles past me, thank God."

Which could only mean, McMahon thought, that he had taken the measure of Priscilla Phelan. "I'll go, I'll go," he said.

He saw a difference in the woman the minute he walked into the room. Her red hair was drawn back and bound in a clasp behind her head where normally she let it go, a wild mane she tossed from around her face while she talked. Nor had she made up her face in the usual way, her eyes shadowed wells, her lips a wounded pucker. Now, wearing no makeup at all, she revealed herself a woman with good natural features, and he wondered which face she wore for Phelan, trying to coax him into her bed, for this was the problem about which she had been coming to him off and on for several weeks.

"You ought to have called before you came," he said.

She made no apology. Nor did she bat her eyes or go through any of the phony posturing that had so put him off her. He had suspected from the beginning that she came to him because he was the best-looking priest she could find. There were times during their sessions when he thought she was getting sexual enjoyment out of describing to him her husband's hangups. "Father, I've lied to you."

"Well," he said, looking down at her, his arms folded, "you're not the first person who has lied to me, and I don't suppose I'm the first person you have lied to."

"That's true, Father. I've also lied to Dan."

"To your husband." He said the words to curtail the intimacy implicit in the use of the name instead of the relationship, man and wife.

"I've been with another man."

"For how long?"

"Several times."

"Over how long a period?"

"Two weeks or so. Please, Father, don't keep looking at me. If I came to you in the confessional you wouldn't."

"It was your choice of where you came to me, Mrs. Phelan," he said, but he went to the window. In their previous conversation it had taken an act of will on his part not to flee her eyes. "When were you here last?"

"Wednesday night."

"Why did you come if you knew you were gong to lie to me?"

"I still wanted to help Dan . . . my husband."

McMahon tried to remember how this conversation had gone on Wednesday night. He could not sort it out from their previous meetings. "I don't quite understand that," he said.

She got up and with a stride the very self-assurance of which he could feel disarming him, walked to the parlor door and closed it. She came and stood beside him. "It's your fault I'm in this mess, Father McMahon. I don't mean you did anything on purpose. God forbid! But the more we talked, it made me wild. Is that a sin? I can't help it. It's the way I'm made, that's all."

"You should not have come to me then," he said. "There are other priests in the parish." He retreated to the little table with the Donnegal shawl over it, angry with her, angrier with himself. He was sure she still was not telling the truth. But that she was trying to tell it now, he had to admit and to deal with. "Or better—most women in your position would have gone to someone in another parish entirely."

"Most women wouldn't go to the priest at all. They'd be ashamed. I like being a woman. I like what I feel." The color had come into her cheeks, a color that made the eyes eloquent as no makeup could.

For the first time he felt a sincere compassion. Perversely, this enabled him to deal with her more severely. "Sit down here at the table and listen to me for a minute." He waited and then seated himself opposite her. "Let's try to be honest with one another. Why did you come to me? Let's dispose of that first."

"Because I thought, he's a priest who would understand."

"Is that the whole truth of it?"

She rested her elbow on the table, her hand, scrubbed clean and without the nail polish, at her cheek so that briefly he was reminded of the hand of the dying man—just in the sensitive use of it. "I'm pretty well educated, Father. I read a lot. There's a bar I used to go with Dan to. Now I go alone when he goes off on his own, promoting some scheme or other, God knows. I sit there and talk with people I've got a feeling for, people who can't get where they want to go. I mean they want to be writers, they're taking polls on the telephone. They're painters . . ." She made a gesture as though to brush the hair away from her face, forgetting that she had fastened it at the back. "I forgot what I started to say."

"Why you came to me in the first place."

"Because you're a musician."

McMahon felt both stunned and humbled.

"Oh, that isn't the whole truth either. Who knows the whole truth about anything, about anybody including yourself? Myself, I mean. I told you the first time I came to see you that I loved Dan, that I wanted him. I know, you don't want to hear that again." Her eyes had caught his in flight.

"You are wrong," he said. She was not wrong: he could feel himself tensing against the repetition of futile intimacies, but he said what he thought was now necessary. "If that's the way you can get at the problem, tell it again."

"No, I won't. I won't talk about Dan. I think I know now what I was doing here though I didn't mean to at first, I was trying to get you going. But that was because I needed to know if I could. Can you understand that?"

"I think so," he said quietly.

"You're a funny one, you know. I got the idea you liked it."

"That was an unwarranted assumption," he said and stared her down. Many a female he had stared down, but most of them were adolescent schoolgirls and easily frightened out of—or into—their fantasies.

"The man I was with is dead," she said flatly.

McMahon let the words rest in silence. He had expected them. What silenced him within himself was that both he and Priscilla Phelan had talked these few minutes as though the death had not occurred.

"The police came. I went with them and identified him as the person I'd rented a back room to. I gave them my extra key. Do I have to tell them, Father? They'll be asking. About me and him, I mean."

"You will have to judge its relevance."

"It's not only me—it might hurt Dan."

He refrained from saying that she should have thought of that earlier. "In what way? Does your husband know of the relationship?"

"I'm not sure, Father. He could have been guessing. When I stopped trying to do what you told me to do . . ."

"Helping him make love to you," McMahon said out.

She nodded. "When I stopped all that—when I just lay there like a whore last night, that turned him on." She broke then, open as even she had never been and spewed out the bitterness. "When I didn't want him he was like a bull. Christ, Father! What's the matter with us?"

"Something I don't think I'm capable of healing," McMahon said. "Maybe, just maybe, it will heal itself— your marriage, given a chance now. It's much too simple for me to say. And I could have been wrong in counseling you the way I did. By trying to provoke his manhood, you may have been taking it away from him."

"It sure is simple that way, Father. But what's inside me isn't simple any more. It's closed up like this." She clenched her fist.

"Time, time," he said, "and prayer. That's the greatest opener I know."

"Maybe for you. For me it's like sucking my thumb. Or something else I won't go into now. It makes me forget for a while, but it doesn't settle anything."

"You said Dan suspected the affair you were having with this man."

She smiled a little and sounded almost wistful. "You make it sound so important."

"Wasn't it important to you at the time?"

"No, Father. I'm sorry, but I'm trying to tell you the truth. You want even sin to be romantic."

"Especially sin," he snapped to cover his chagrin that she should mock him.

"It wasn't love. It was just plain sex. I seduced him. You won't have any trouble believing that, will you? You know, most of the tenants in my building don't buy this business of going to the priest every time somebody gets into somebody else's bed. They talk about it on the stoop, in the kitchen. It's the way they are. Maybe that's why I can't live with them.

"Last night after Dan got through proving himself, he got up and dressed again. He said to me, 'Now you got something new to tell your friends.' 'I don't tell them anything,' I said. 'That's not the message I get from them.' 'Then they're lying,' I said. 'Are they, Pris? About the bearded gentleman in the back room? Who is he? What is he?' 'He's a man,' I shouted and Dan said, 'So now you have two men, lucky girl.' He went out then, Father, and I haven't seen him since."

"Have you told any of this to the police?" McMahon said after a moment.

"Not much, except about Dan not being home. They'll start asking. It was mostly Gus they wanted to know about."

"Your husband has been away overnight before, hasn't he? If a job took him out of town?"

"Yes, but he's not on one now."

McMahon yielded then to an impulse he had ben trying to repress. "Tell me something about the man—Muller."

"He was murdered this morning in that condemned building on the other side of Tenth Avenue."

"I know. I was with him when he died. Carlos Morales came and got me."

She thought about that. "Now I understand. Carlos . . . He loved kids. I wouldn't be surprised if he's got some of his own somewhere. He'd make nice babies with the right woman. A gentle person . . . but *with* it." She was silent for a moment, her eyes thoughtful. McMahon waited. He knew quite a lot about her, some things she wanted him to know and some he had learned by inadvertence. He knew that she was thirty-two, the daughter of a broken marriage who had spent her childhood and adolescence in a convent boarding school, and then, when her father died, her mother had brought her home to live with her in the tenement building she now owned herself: a clash of environments if he had ever known one. She and Phelan had been married when she was nineteen and pregnant for the first and last time. The child had been stillborn.

"It's funny, Father," she went on finally, "but I can't talk about him that way, me, the big talker."

"But you said it wasn't important," he chided gently.

"I guess it was just that I didn't want it to be important. I liked him a lot. I don't even think Gus Muller was his right name. Gust—I always forgot the 't' and he liked it. We met in the Duminy Bar I told you about on Ninth Avenue. He needed a room cheap and a job he wouldn't have to pay taxes on. So we settled on him painting the apartment." She looked at her hands where she had clasped them tightly on the table. "I slept with him that night. That sounds pretty raw, doesn't it, Father?"

"Since you say it yourself," he murmured. "What else? What did he do before he started drifting?"

She shook her head. "He wouldn't tell me. 'I am who you think I am. That's all you need to know. And when we're together, it's all I need to know.' And the funny thing is, he was right. I didn't care who he was. We were like two people cut loose in space, only I wasn't afraid."

"And yet you came to me Wednesday night and pretended you were still trying to help your husband."

"I wasn't pretending. I'd made up my mind—for Dan's sake—to keep on trying even if I didn't care any more."

"Have you any idea what Muller was doing in the building where he died?"

"No. I used to hear him go out very early in the morning—dawn. He'd work for me in the afternoons—and other places. He'd come home sometimes walking along with Carlos or carrying him on his shoulders. Home . . . a shirt, a razor, a toothbrush, and a pair of clean shorts hung up to dry on the back of the chair."

"If the women gossiped to your husband they will to the police too, you know."

"No. You're wrong about that too, Father. They wouldn't tell the police the time of day. It's up to me what I tell them. Me and Dan."

It was she who was wrong: one of her neighbors had already told the police that Phelan did not like Muller.

"They're bound to ask questions," he said, "the man living in your house."

"It's a back room, separate. Its own door. The john's in the hall."

They were both avoiding the real question. Phelan's capacity for violence. McMahon made up his mind he would not be the one to bring it into the open. "You ought to go home and wait for your husband."

"What if he doesn't come home? The police will want to know why."

"Could you tell them why?"

"No, but . . ."

"I'd just leave it at no, Mrs. Phelan."

"I will, but they won't, Father. Dan has an assault record. He cut up a man with a bottle once."

"Over you?"

"Hell, no," she said bitterly. "Over a dog that lifted his leg on Dan's shoe."

five minutes past five McMahon approached the precinct adquarters. He noticed that one of the two white globes at hung on either side of the entrance had been smashed. was odd, the association, but he thought of the words, ove Power," scratched on the sidewalk outside the doomed building. Not so odd. One was as sure a sign of the times as the other. He also saw Carlos and his mother before they saw him. Mrs. Morales gave the boy a push out the door ahead of her, but then, seeing the priest on the steps, she caught her son's curly head and hugged him against her. Carlos responded as limply to affection as he did to abuse.

"He's a good boy, Father, but sometimes I don't know what to do with him." When she spoke the gold of her teeth glittered.

The priest ruffled the boy's hair with his hand.

"His brother, he is the bad one." She jerked her head toward the station, which indicated that the older boy was in now with the police. "He hates the police. Why? They have a job to do like everybody else. He would like them to beat him, that's how much he hates them. He was the same with his father. I do not understand. If you speak to him, Father, tell him, please, to be more polite?" The pleading of her voice was as ancient as motherhood.

"I will," McMahon said. What he did not say was that Pedrito Morales had little more regard for priests than he did for the police. Or his own father. But she knew that too. The conversation was its own kind of ritual, not entirely false, but the forms barely holding together.

26

At the bottom of the steps she turned and called after him: "Father, he was a good man, Mr. Muller. Everybody wants he should have a nice funeral. You know?" By the rubbing together of her fingers she suggested money. "Come to my house, Father. The people liked him. They will all give something." That, he felt, was genuine.

He asked for Brogan at the desk. The sergeant directed him to a room on the second floor. He went up by way of a staircase, the color and smell of which put him in mind of a cheap hotel. The windows were wire-meshed on the outside, sealing in the dirt of generations. He met Brogan and Lieutenant Traynor coming out of the room with Pedrito, a tall, skinny boy of eighteen, sallow and sullen, with a mop of black hair and a scraggle of beard.

The best he could do for him at the moment was to acknowledge an acquaintanceship. "Hello, Pedrito."

The boy nodded curtly.

"Keep your nose clean, young fellow. We'll be watching you," Traynor said.

"Cochinos," Pedrito snarled. Pigs. But by then he had reached the stairs.

"Makes you want to love them, doesn't it?" Traynor said. He went on down the hall.

Brogan led the priest into the interrogation room where an officer was removing the tape from a recorder. They waited until he had left the room.

"So you had to bring Carlos in anyway," McMahon said.

"Si," Brogan said. He searched a folder for the statements he wanted.

McMahon was not to be put off. "Why?"

Brogan shrugged. "The lieutenant didn't like it, not the way the kid told it to us. The doorknobs were what really put him in a flap."

"I don't get it."

"Well, Father, let me put it this way: he questioned the boy on whether Muller had molested him."

McMahon's temper snapped. "Balls."

"Exactly."

"Christ Jesus help us," McMahon said, but he already knew he was being unreasonable. The luring of a child to an abandoned building: it could be construed that way. Even the monsignor's first question was whether the man was a pervert.

Brogan half-sat on the desk. He indicated the chair to the priest. "What is it that bugs you, Father? You know yourself that a kid like Carlos, there's nothing he's going to learn from us he didn't know from the street already."

McMahon sat down and took in hand his own typed statement. What Brogan said was true: trying to shield the innocence of a child in Carlos' environment was almost as impossible as the restoration of virginity. He read the statement and signed it.

"But you're right," Brogan said. "That wasn't Muller's trouble."

"What was?"

Brogan shrugged. "Mrs. Phelan? Or vice versa. I have a notion she was hot for him. There's gossip in the building. Even we can get to it. She picked him up in a bar, nestled him down in her back room. Like charity begins at home. Where was Phelan through all this? Where *is* Phelan?"

And what's his problem? McMahon kept the thought to himself, but he suspected Brogan was doing the same thing. He asked, "Is Pedrito in the clear?"

"As far as the homicide, he has to be. He works on a machine assembly line. Twenty witnesses to where he was from six A.M. to three this afternoon. And he wasn't a chum of the victim. That was Carlos' idea. To a kid, I guess, everybody over fifteen is the same age, especially if they come to his birthday party. They all drank wine that night and it was then Muller got the idea of building a house of doors for the youngster. Pedrito went with him. If he gets into no worse trouble than swiping doors, I'll settle."

McMahon said, "Why are you a cop, Brogan?"

The young detective colored. "To stay out of the draft. I'll take my law and order straight, Father."

The priest was not sure why, but he felt a kind of respect for Brogan saying it.

"Phelan has an assault record, by the way," Brogan added.

"Was he at the birthday party too?"

"No, but Mrs. Phelan was."

"It makes you wonder why there was gossip, if she's so popular with her tenants," McMahon said, "and they're not notoriously cooperative with the police, are they?"

"It's pretty simple, Father—it's not the infidelity, if that's what it is. Homicide is something you can get put away for a long time. They don't like Phelan."

That had to be it, McMahon realized. Priscilla Phelan had not calculated the relative values of her Spanish-speaking friends. "Do you want me to go over Carlos' story?"

"It won't be necessary, unless you want to see it. You can go over to the house if you want to—I'll fix it up—if you want to see his things. There's not much there. He was traveling light, wherever he came from. A sign painter by his identification."

McMahon shook his head: he did not want to go near the Phelan apartment.

Brogan tapped his statement with a pencil. "I just thought by this you might be interested."

"I am," McMahon said. "He got to me and I'm not sure why. Was it his courage? He was ready to die, but it was as though that was because he wanted to live, to live right up to and over the threshold. And he said he would like to know me. That always sets a man up, doesn't it?"

"It sure does, Father."

"There was more to him than what he left in that room, I feel pretty sure of that."

"Then have a look at his things."

"No. That's your business. But you're right. I'd like to know."

"I'll keep in touch with you, Father. Thanks for coming in."

* * *

It was a good time of day, McMahon thought, reaching the street. Next to dawn he loved it the best, the last hours of the sun when its heat was spent but a golden haze hung over the city. The youngsters were playing stickball, and great fat women leaned out their windows watching for their men to come home from work. There were flags in the windows of almost half the apartments. No college deferments here. Brogan was not a young man whose insight should be underestimated: he would not say to many people in this neighborhood that he joined the force to avoid the army.

Crossing Ninth Avenue he decided to walk downtown a few blocks to Ferguson and Kelly's funeral parlor. It was no new thing to him, trying to arbitrate the costs of a funeral: he generally did well until the family arrived to select the casket. This part of town, where the street markets commenced, was predominantly Italian. Sausages and cheeses hung in the windows over stacked canisters of olive oil, two-quart tins of tomatoes. The produce was all outdoors. The people were noisy and friendly and a priest was accepted as one of themselves, neither feared nor revered. It was a strange place for Ferguson and Kelly, but as he thought about it, he could not name an Italian in the undertaking business. That they left to the morbid Irish. But obviously in Italy Italians buried Italians. Could the circumstance here be the dominance of the Irish in the church? Since Muller was not a Catholic, or so he assumed, he would have to see Ferguson, a man he took to be of Scotch-Irish antecedence. He would rather have negotiated with Kelly. As he opened the door setting off the muted chimes, he wished he had telephoned. A typical McMahonism: taking the steps first and weighing the consequences only when he had no choice but to live up to them.

A half hour later he headed uptown again, a set of if-or-and figures in his pocket and a stiff Scotch whisky in his stomach. The whisky roused in him a feeling of kinship with every man on the street, and he went over in his mind the lines of his sermon. They were not so bad after all, he decided, with even a touch of poetry to them. Long ago the monsignor had said to him, "Remember, you're not addressing the sacred congregation in Rome. Simple truths are the most eloquent. Sincerity, that's the key." Which put him in mind of politicians and brought him round full circle to the banal again. Priests and politicians. He felt as restless as the birds scratching in the gutters. His spirits fell as low. He had not yet read his office of the day. That and music and his morning Mass were his refuge. All having little to do with the world around him. It was not that the world was too much with him, but that he was too much with the world. He wondered what Muller would have thought of that distinction.

The pawnbroker was closing the iron grill across his shop windows as McMahon approached. The grill gave the shop more distinction than the merchandise warranted, the grill and the three golden balls newly painted, and the sign, Gothic-lettered in fresh gold leaf—or so it appeared in the slanting rays of the sun: A. ROSENBERG.

McMahon thought at once of Muller, a sign painter, but he also thought of the curiosity of the Gothic lettering of the name. He was himself familiar with the typeface from liturgical books, but ninety-nine out of a hundred would have to puzzle the letters to get the name. Ninth Avenue Gothic. He greeted the pawnbroker. They knew each other by sight, and there was a placard in the window announcing the girls' choir concert.

"I'm curious, Mr. Rosenberg." He pointed to the sign. "Why in those letters?"

Rosenberg looked up and shaded his eyes. "Beautiful, eh?"

McMahon agreed.

"Why not? It isn't the phone book. The whole neighborhood knows Rosenberg. They don't need the sign. Only Rosenberg needs it. I like it, that's why."

"Was it a man named Muller who painted it?"

"Would you believe me, Father, I don't know his last name? A beard and beautiful hands. I always notice hands."

"He's dead, you know," the priest said.

He had not expected the man's reaction, the little moan of a personal pain and the mouth working under the gray mustache. Rosenberg put his hand to the grating and held onto it.

"I'm sorry," McMahon said, "I didn't realize he was a friend."

"When?"

"This morning." McMahon told him the circumstances.

"Come inside." He made a gesture to let the gate stand open. "Leave it. I don't have to keep union hours, thank God." He led the way through the shop to his desk in the back and lit the green-shaded lamp above it. He pulled out the swivel chair and made the priest take it. The desk, an ancient rolltop, was littered with papers, letters in foreign handwriting, some in Yiddish, or so McMahon presumed from a glance. "Coffee? Or a glass of cognac, Father."

"A little cognac, thank you."

"He liked the cognac, too, let me tell you. But he liked also the coffee. But most of all he liked to talk."

"I'd have thought that," the priest said.

Rosenberg got his glasses from the desk drawer and put them on. "Let me show you." He looked more like a scholar than a pawnbroker as he went to a shelf and looked up. His white hair fringed the collar of his coat. He started to take a large book from among several on the shelf, then changed his mind, and with a sweep of his hand, he abandoned them to McMahon's own scrutiny. "They are his, Bosch, Vermeer, the Italians. He did not like the Italians except for Botticelli."

McMahon took down the Bosch while Rosenberg went to a cabinet and brought out the bottle and two stemmed glasses. The book was so heavy McMahon had to lay it on the desk to open it. It revealed nothing but Bosch, but that was quite a lot, the contrasts of good and evil, and as in most things, he thought, the evil figures were by far the most interesting. There was no name, no mark at all in the front pages, only the smudges of use.

Rosenberg cleared a place on the desk, put the glasses down and poured the brandy, twice as much for the priest as he poured for himself. "Oh, yes. He liked to talk. I did not understand half of what he was talking about, but I liked to listen to him. I liked to listen," he repeated. "And now it is one more voice not to listen to." He lifted his glass. "To him, *shalom*."

"*Shalom*," McMahon said. Peace.

He took a sip of the brandy and then put the book back on the shelf. He took down another volume and looked at the flyleaves: nothing. "How long have you had these, Mr. Rosenberg?" What he realy wanted to ask at the moment was how much it would cost him to buy them if they were not redeemed.

"He brought in the Bosch maybe three weeks ago. The others in between. I have no claim on them, Father. It was a matter of some place to keep them for the time being. 'I don't like possessions,' he said. 'Why do people collect things? Because they cannot bear to be alone, alone with themselves.' Something like that. He was always saying things like that."

McMahon examined the books one by one while the pawnbroker was talking. Not one gave any clue to its ownership.

"He came in that first day and said, 'I am a one-man crusade to clean up the store fronts on Ninth Avenue. You clean the windows and I will paint.' 'How much?' I said. 'For a half day's work, what it costs me to live for a day.' He did not look as though he lived extravagantly. I paid him ten dollars and the paint, and it was to me a valuable investment to meet the man. He was a kind of salesman like that, you know? I was the first customer he worked it on, I found out afterwards. Next he went to the drugstore on the corner. That was a disgrace. He showed me as a model. A half dozen shops in all maybe. Until now. But I am thinking, where did he come from? Could it be there are little islands like this all over New York? Fresh paint and clean windows? How long would he have stayed? And why did he have to leave . . . that way." Rosenberg fell silent. He sipped the brandy, smacked his lips and nodded at his own thoughts.

McMahon returned to the chair. The brandy seared its way down his throat and seemed to grab at his stomach. He was reminded of the hour of the day. He had been late for lunch. Miss Lalor would be in a temper if he was late for dinner also. Then he thought how truly unimportant were Miss Lalor's tempers.

Rosenberg looked at him. "He was sitting here where I am one day, and I was there at the desk and he said to me: 'Rembrandt would have liked you. Right as you are, the light, the junk, the cupboards, everything. He would have made of you one of his famous Jews.' And I said to him, on the chance it would bring him out, you know: 'Rembrandt is already dead and I am not yet a famous Jew.' I looked him in the eye when I said it, but he only laughed and shook his head. All the same, Father, I think he was a painter of more than signs and store fronts."

"I think so too," McMahon said.

After a moment Rosenberg said, "You will tell the police you were here?"

"I shall have to."

"What can I tell them, a man I knew only by the name of Gus? Gust. He liked the 't' on the end of it. I do not like to think they will take his books away. I like to think he will come back for them."

"He won't."

"Or somebody then to talk to the way we talked."

"I will not tell them about the books. That is up to you," McMahon said. He would have to examine his own conscience on his moment of covetousness of them. Long ago he had wanted to be a painter even more than he had wanted to be a musician, but even less than he had wanted to be a priest. "Did he ever talk about himself?" He knew the answer before asking it. If he had, Rosenberg would have said so.

The pawnbroker shook his head.

"Not even where he lived, where he was bringing the books from? Or why?"

"No, not a word personal. Oblique: it was a word he liked, but he was talking about light, the light of a painter."

"If the police are told about them, they will want to check if they were stolen."

"He did not steal them," Rosenberg said vehemently.

"You are judging by our values, my friend," McMahon said. "And you and I both know now he was a very unconventional man."

"That is true, but even looking at it from a practical point of view, Father, it would be easier to steal a hippopotamus than Hieronymus Bosch."

McMahon laughed and finished his brandy. He held up his hand to stay the pawnbroker from pouring more. "I must go. If there is no family claim on his body, there will probably be a service at Ferguson and Kelly's."

"When?"

"That will depend on the police, I suppose. The autopsy. I will see that the newspapers get a notice."

"What kind of a service?"

"That's the question, isn't it? It's the people in the building where he lived who want it."

"Funerals are always for the living," Rosenberg said, getting to his feet with the priest. "I think he would have agreed to that."

"I will play some Bach on the organ," McMahon said.

"And Mahler. He liked Mahler."

McMahon said, "Gustave Muller, Gustav Mahler." The association had crossed his mind the first time he heard the complete name. He and Rosenberg looked at each other. "So it is possible we don't even know his real name."

"I am thinking, Father, what I am going to do: I am going to sit down and try to write the things I remember we talked about. It will not sound very much, the way I write it. I have tried to write before, and my mind it becomes a moth just trying to get at the light. But I will try and I will give it to you. Who knows? Maybe you and I can talk also."

"I would like that," the priest said.

At the door of the shop they shook hands. McMahon remembered that it was Friday. "Good *shabbos*," he said.

"*Gut shabbos*." Rosenberg squinted up at the sky. "It will be a fine sunset."

5

It had been McMahon's intention to go directly home. But then that had been his intention when he had left the precinct station house well over an hour earlier. He found himself walking toward the sunset. Scotch and brandy and Gustave Muller. Benediction and rosary at eight, a sermon to be got into his head, Muller out. He paused at the parapet beneath which lay the railroad tracks and beyond which the West Side Highway arched against the sky. Every approaching car caught an instant of sunset in its windshield, passed, and seemed no more than a beetle on a rampart. He turned and walked back on the street where Muller had died. The rush of suburb-going traffic was over, the street again a silent wilderness, bulldozers and cranes the dinosaurs of the era. The one lone building stood, its walls raw brick where the walls it once met had been shorn away. At the very top, the windows shone like golden eyes.

He paused where the uniformed policeman stood by the basement grill and exchanged a few words with him. "Love Power" had been all but wiped out with the shuffle of many feet. At the top of the steps the double doorway was open. "Mind if I go up, officer?"

"I guess it'd be all right, Father. They're all through up there. Jut stay away from the basement."

"Believe me, I will."

A house without doors, he noticed, climbing one flight of dusty stairs after the other. To have stolen the doorknobs Muller would have needed to be around for a while. And he was, of course. Carlos had said that, the man coming

down when he called him. The turn-of-the-century gas fix-
tures were still in the hallways, and there were patches of
a floral-patterned wallpaper where the paint had chipped
away. On every landing he noticed a clutter of tinfoil and
burnt-out photography bulbs. The police had gone over the
building well. The roof hatch had been tilted to let in air.
When he reached the fifth and final floor the room to the
west was suffused with light, the blearing X's had been
removed from the windows. There were spatters of paint
on the floor, and squares of raw wood where bits of the
surface had been cut out, he suspected for laboratory study.
So the police too would now presume him to have been an
easel painter as well as the painter of Mrs. Phelan's walls.
Northern light was painters' light, and in the mornings here
Muller would have had the best of it. Now, with the sun
having gone down, the sky was changing fast, holding briefly
the red and yellow tints, then almost palpably letting them
go, yielding to the darker strokes of night. The room was
utterly bare. Silence and peace: he could feel it. He found
it himself only at the altar when he was no longer himself,
at the moment of the transubstantiation. His conscience told
him that he must go, but the wish to wait for night was very
strong.

"Father McMahon?" The voice halloed up the stairwell.

He thought it would be Brogan and went to the top of
the stairs.

"Stay there. I'm coming up."

McMahon went to the west window and waited. Torn
wisps of cloud held the last pinks and lemon of the sunset.

"Some spot he found for himself, wouldn't you say,
Father?"

"How did he find it?"

"We've been asking the same question. The building
belongs to an old crank who wouldn't sell it to the devel-
opers. They went ahead without him, starting the wreckers
next door. They wouldn't give him the ground to shore up
his walls. The city condemned. The building's going but he

still won't sell the land. It's in the courts and it's been in the papers, but he never heard of Gustave Muller."

"But the abandoned building could have been what attracted Muller to the neighborhood," McMahon said. "What did you find in this room?"

"An old army cot and three more doorknobs."

"Nothing else?"

"A few spatters of paint. He could have decorated the kid's doorknobs up here."

"He'd have needed a brush and paint," McMahon said. "It wasn't here."

"And nothing like that where he lived?"

Brogan shook his head. "No Phelan yet either."

"And no weapon," McMahon said after a moment.

"It was a square-edged blade. Maybe a narrow chisel."

Or a palette knife, McMahon thought, but he did not say so.

"He cleaned up a few store fronts on Ninth Avenue," Brogan said. "A real eccentric, like they say."

McMahon felt relieved of having to tell him of his conversation with Rosenberg. But to compensate—his own conscience, he thought afterward—he reminded the detective of Muller's last words.

"I was going over your statement again, Father. That's some pretty fancy talk between you and him. What do you think he meant when he said he'd taken the knife from his killer?"

"I suppose I took it to mean that the man was not dangerous to anyone else."

"That's the way I read it, and that's pure crap, Father. Unless he killed himself and got somebody to get rid of the weapon for him."

"Who?"

Brogan shrugged. "And why? Nobody who had any sense would touch it. That leaves the kid."

"Carlos? I'm sure he ran all the way from here to the rectory."

"So am I. I think he told it the way it was."

McMahon could hardly read the dial hand on his watch. "I've got to get home."

"We've canvassed all the big art galleries, Father, on the chance he painted something besides balls and walls. But maybe they wouldn't know him under that name. His Social Security number's fake. He was on the run from something. We'll find out."

McMahon remembered his earlier mission that evening. "How long will you keep the body?"

"We've got the facilities. Till somebody claims it."

"The tenants of 987 would like a funeral service."

"A wake?"

"I suppose you could call it that. I've inquired about the costs at Ferguson and Kelly."

"So you need the mortal remains. I'll speak to Traynor. It's something the newspapers would pick up. The publicity might help us."

"I want to think about it first," McMahon said. "Hold off speaking to Traynor." The whole idea now became repugnant to him.

At the top of the stairs Brogan said, "You're right, Father. Somebody would be on our necks for it, some organization for the rights of corpses." A few steps down, he paused. "Hah! I remember a song my grandfather used to sing when he'd get a few drinks in him . . . 'If this wake goes on a minute, sure the corpse he must be in it. You'll have to get me drunk to keep me dead.' That's the end of it. I forget the beginning."

How fortunate, McMahon thought.

On the Street Brogan asked: "Are you off duty now, Father?"

"No. I've taken French leave."

"What does that mean?"

McMahon rubbed the back of his neck. "I guess it means AWOL. It's Irish. I don't remember ever saying it before myself."

"I check out in a half hour. I was going to suggest, if you're free, have a meal and a couple of drinks with me."

"Where?"

"Downtown. The Village maybe."

"He wasn't the Village type," the priest said, although God knew, he said it on shallow grounds.

"Maybe he wasn't, Father, but I was thinking about his killer. And I could use a good excuse for a few hours on the town. What do you say?"

"If you don't mind starting with Benediction and rosary. I'll be free after that."

"In mufti, Father."

"The best mufti I have," McMahon said.

6

It was only after McMahon had resisted the temptation to take the steak bone in his fingers that he remembered, "Holy God," he said, "it's Friday."

"Well, it's not a sin any more, is it?" Brogan wiped his fingers in his napkin. He had not been inhibited about taking the bone in hand.

"No, not for you, but a priest should hold to it."

"But tonight you're on French leave—was that it?—and if I know the French..." The young policeman rolled his eyes. His cheeks were flushed. They had had two stiff drinks before dinner.

McMahon brushed the crumbs from the lapel of his sport jacket. "I was trying to think where that term could have come from."

"World War I?"

"Much earlier, I think. From the time of Napoleon, I shouldn't be surprised, when the French fleet turned back from the west coast of Ireland and left Wolfe Tone in the lurch."

"That's the French for you," Brogan said solemnly.

"There was a MacMahon, a general in the French army in those days."

"Was there now? Were you related?"

McMahon grinned. He was aware that after the drinks both of them were falling into a brogue of sorts. "Well, there were Wild Geese in the family, I'm told, Irish soldiers fighting in the French army."

"Ah, yes. We're a race that fights best when the cause is somebody else's. Wouldn't you say that, Joseph?"

McMahon flinched inwardly at the policeman's use of his first name, the deferential young man of the afternoon. He laughed to cover his pulling-in in case it showed. But Brogan would not have noticed. McMahon would not be the first priest he had taken on the town. He said, "Well, we fight best for lost causes, and no man's our hero until we've made a martyr out of him." Nonsense, he thought. Poetic nonsense.

"Brian Boru and Kevin Barry?" Brogan suggested.

"I'm not sure about Brian Boru," McMahon said. "Shall we have coffee or another drink?"

"Irish coffee?"

"It's too early in the night for that," McMahon said.

"You're a man after my own heart." Brogan reached for his wallet. "Let's have a drink somewhere else."

"Down the middle," McMahon said of the check.

"Not tonight. Who knows? Before it's out we may turn up something that'll put the city in debt for our tab."

McMahon said nothing. He did not know which he liked the least: carousing on Brogan or on the taxpayer. But with the ten dollars he had borrowed from the monsignor on the way out and his own two, he would not pick up many tabs. Remember your prerogatives and not your pride, the old man had bidden him, not for the first time.

But McMahon enjoyed himself all the same. The streets were alive with youth and music, purveyors and flowers and chestnuts, carters of cameras and souvenirs, papier maché and art nouveau, sailors on leave and cops on vigil. He loved the young people, beards, beads and begonias, and if he had had his way, he and Brogan would have sat astride an old Morgan car parked near MacDougal Street, and he'd have conducted the singing himself. ". . . Now don't you know that's not the way to end the war . . ." a young troubadour sang to the off-key strum of his guitar.

"Beautiful!" McMahon shouted. "Sing it again."

A whole chorus of young people did.

A fire truck approached, its bell clanging. The youngsters pushed back from the street, but coming abreast of them and making the wide turn even wider than necessary, the fireman gave a deafening blast with his bullhorn. A lepre-chaun of a boy cupped his hands around his mouth and shouted after the truck: "Yankee, go home!"

McMahon threw back his head and laughed as he had not laughed for a long time. A shaggy-haired girl came up to him and held out a string of beads. McMahon stooped and allowed her to put them around his neck. He offered her money but she would not take it. The Yankee-go-home boy came up behind her and said, "Excuse me, miss, but your skirt is showing."

Finally Brogan got McMahon away. He was looking for a particular bar. When he found it and they went in, he said, "My feet need a rest. Let's sit in a booth."

McMahon too was glad to sit down. He was trying to remember a line of Yeats. He got it the moment he stretched his legs under the table. "There midnight's all a-glimmer and noon a purple glow." So was the bar. There was this to be said for a priest's night out: it was so rare an occasion, the whole laughing world seemed to join him. With a few drinks McMahon became a democrat, as by the light of day assuredly he was not. He thought of Father Purdy, poor little Purdy, obsequious as a snail, pulling in, poking out on his way to the throne of God.

"I need a drink," he said.

"I'll go get them myself," Brogan said. The bar was crowded.

He drank more than he ought to, McMahon knew, and like Miniver Cheevy, he had reasons. Miniver Cheevy, child of scorn . . . something about the Medici. He would have sinned incessantly, could he have been one.

There was a small commotion at the bar before Brogan pushed his way through the men and returned with the drinks. His color was as high as the lights were low, and he was cursing under his breath. It was only then that McMahon realized they were in a homosexual hangout.

"What did you come in here for then?"

"On a hunch," Brogan said. He ruffled his shoulders and then settled back, seating himself so that he too could view the bar. "It takes all kinds," he said, "and sure the whisky comes out of the same keg."

"So do we all," McMahon said, aware of the sententiousness even as he said it. *"Slainte."* It was the one word of Gaelic he knew. He touched his glass to Brogan's.

"Did you ever know an Irish fag, Joseph?"

"Any number, but most of them in clergy's petticoats."

Brogan was shocked, for all his worldliness. The double standard had just quadrupled. "Is that a fact?" he murmured, but not believing it for a moment.

McMahon stared at the men at the bar, the tight little behinds in the snug narrow-legged pants. "Poor bastards," he said, and threw down his drink.

"You'll go for the next one yourself and see how you like it."

McMahon said, "I'll have the next one on the road home."

But Brogan sipped. He was in no hurry. He took a match packet from his pocket, and played with it, folding one match, then another into a fan. "Go on, get yourself a drink, Joseph. I dare you."

"Since you put it that way, I might."

McMahon approached the bar flanking it so that he came up last man where it curved to the wall. He glanced down the row of faces: young, aging, delicate, tired, gay . . . gay, gay, gay, but there wasn't a cruel face among them. But where that night would he have seen a face that he thought cruel? It was a second or two after his scanning of them all that he realized he knew one of the men. He turned abruptly from the bar, only to all but bump into Brogan who had come up behind him.

"Sit down," the detective said. "I'll fetch your drink."

"I don't want one."

"You'll need it," Brogan said. "Sit down."

McMahon did as he was told. The night had lost its glow and so had he. He watched Brogan fake amiability with the men, and then looked away. What had he expected from a cop? The taxpayers' money. He picked up the fanned match packet. Pierre's Unique. That's where they were, in Pierre's Unique. Eunuch, unique. Christ Jesus forgive me. He tore one match after another from the packet. Brogan returned.

"Which one is he?"

McMahon almost involuntarily put his hand to where at another time he would be wearing the collar.

"The high turtleneck sweater?"

"That's he."

"I'll be back in a minute," Brogan said, and then before leaving, "I picked those up when I was talking to his wife." He indicated the matches.

"Congratulations," McMahon said.

Brogan went to the phone booth between the doors to the rest rooms. McMahon watched him over his shoulder until he had dialed. Then he stared at the back of Daniel Phelan, the narrow back and the skinny hips and the run-down heels with the hole in one sock. The informer priest. Phelan, he knew, had not seen him. He was tempted to run. No, you'll stick it out, he told himself, and learn a little deeper how the troubled man confronts his trouble. He was, he knew, absolving Phelan of the murder rather more for reasons of his own self-disgust, and he was remembering, despite the wish not to, Priscilla Phelan's words to him that day, "Like a bull last night, Father, when I no longer wanted him . . ." He shuddered. With what? His own sexuality? He lifted the glass and studied the whisky. You keep it in a bottle, Joseph. Corked up tight. Up tight.

Brogan came from the phone and slipped easily into the booth. His eyes were bright with excitement. "We've earned our night on the town, Joseph."

McMahon forced a tight-lipped smile.

The policeman leaned closer, touching the priest's glass with his. "Look, man. It's only for questioning. And it's better now than later for him. You know that."

McMahon grunted assent. He drank down his drink. He had not meant to. It had lost its savor.

"Take it easy on that, Joseph. We've a long ways to go when this bit of work is over."

"How long till they get here?"

Brogan shrugged.

"Do we have to wait?" He hated himself for saying it, but it had occurred to him that he might be expected to take part in the arrest.

"Just to make sure," Brogan said. "Our work is all done—unless he tries a runout before they get here."

But Phelan made no move, scarcely even to raise his glass to his lips or to shift his weight one foot to the other. He might not even know Muller was dead, unless . . . What Brogan did not know was Phelan's performance with his wife the night before. Was that what the poor devil now was pondering? The fear to go home lest it be expected of him again? McMahon made a restless gesture, a sweep of his hand that upset his glass. The ice tinkled out.

"Easy, Joseph. You don't want to call attention."

They sat in silence, the hands of the Roman-numeraled clock above the back bar spanning the long slow minutes from eleven-three to eleven-eighteen.

When the two detectives walked in the men nearest the doorway, glancing round, stiffened a little, straightened a little, and then there was almost silence, talk and laughter cut mid-sound. There would have to have been some signal between Brogan and them, McMahon thought, but he did not see it. They seemed to know Phelan on sight. One on either side of him, they showed their identification. He went out with them without protest except for the motion to pay his check. The bartender waved him on. Had all this happened to him before? McMahon wondered. The resignation of the man was what troubled him. What did he know of Phelan except from Mrs. Phelan? And from the neighbors who didn't like him. He remembered the man's only police record, assault because a dog had lifted his leg on his shoe.

"Well, shall we go?" Brogan said. He could not restrain a little show of expansiveness. "There's a phone call I have to make."

"Make it." McMahon jerked his head toward the phone booth. He dreaded the crawl to the street.

Brogan grinned. "Not here. It would be a desecration."

He was about to get to his feet when the bartender came up to him. He was a big man, broad-shouldered. He jerked his thumb toward the door.

"Roger," Brogan said.

The bartender looked down at McMahon. "You, too, Padre. I can smell the cloth."

"Watch it," Brogan said. "Even a joint like this needs a license."

McMahon got up, again upsetting the glass. This time it broke. "I'm sorry," he said.

But Brogan with the back of his hand deliberately knocked over his own glass on the table.

McMahon got out as best he could with the burden of humiliation and anger. Brogan stood on the curb and stretched to his full height. He rubbed his belly with both hands and drew in several deep breaths. "Now for a telephone. There's a drugstore on the corner." He touched the priest's elbow to turn him in that direction. "You're game, aren't you, Joseph?"

"For what?"

"Aw, come off it, Joseph. They're nice girls, and they're clean. And they'll think you're a cop."

McMahon shook his head. "I've had too much to drink."

"You'll have coffee while I'm on the phone."

He went as far as the drugstore and had the coffee. It was as black as tar, as his own mood.

Brogan came from the phone and ordered coffee for himself. "Do you have any money, Joseph?"

"Twelve dollars."

"Buy a fifth of Scotch. I'll take care of the rest."

McMahon bought the whisky and set the bottle before Brogan on the counter. He was drunker than he had thought and yet he wanted more. He wanted what? Just whisky. Not a woman, not now. Just whisky and the last bitter dregs of the night.

Brogan drank his coffee. "They've a nice little place on Tenth Street. You'll be surprised. Or maybe you won't. They're nice girls."

"You said that."

"I know. But you won't believe me till you meet them." He picked up the bottle, crumpling the paper at the neck, and brandished it. "Tally-ho!"

McMahon did not even know if Brogan was married. He did not want to know. He followed him as though the bottle was a pipe and Brogan the piper. And then as they walked, his the careful walk of the man who knows he is drunk and has to take care of the drunkard in him, he began to say to himself, "Jesus help me, Jesus and Mary, help me. Jesus, Mary and Joseph. . . . Only Joseph can help you." He felt the sweat cold on his brow, on his back, beneath his armpits. As they turned the corner of Sixth Avenue, he heard the rumble of the subway. Students were going down the steps, books under their arms, and the gray of their faces telling of long days' work and nights spent in the classroom.

"Good night, Brogan." He heard a part of himself saying it, and it was almost as though another part of him was surprised. "My apologies to the ladies."

Brogan stood—with the air of a man balancing himself on the top of the world, so that again a part of McMahon wanted to go on with him—and studied the priest for seriousness, for whether or not he wanted to be persuaded. Then he shrugged. "Okay. No hard feelings, Father?"

Father.

"No hard feelings," McMahon said, but he could not bring himself to a false thanksgiving.

7

The first thing McMahon thought of when he awakened in the morning was that walk to the subway entrance. *Only Joseph can help you.* He had never said that before. He sat on the side of the bed, his aching head in his hands, and castigated himself. There were times when he had called on a litany of saints to get him home safely, and once he had pictured himself—or dreamed it—carted home on the back of St. Christopher. On the floor at his feet was his breviary. He had managed his office, just the words, but he had managed it, and he had slept in his own bed. He would have to manage now, for he could not break his fast with an aspirin. He dreaded the first sip of wine at the altar. *God forgive me. Lord, I am not worthy. . . .* He showered and shaved and saw, whether he wanted to or not, the bloodshot eyes of a priest in the mirror. *I will go unto the altar of God, to God who gives joy to my youth:* the new liturgy had taken that from him, but he never entered the sanctuary that the words did not pass through his mind: *to God who gives joy to my youth.* Youth and joy. He was forty years old and the devil was hard on his tracks. And there was Muller again, with the dark spittle on his lips: *Do you believe in him, horns, tail and all?* I believe in evil. Deliver us from evil. Amen, amen, amen.

"Well, Joseph, you've made *The New York Times* as well as the *Daily News*." The monsignor was walking through the hall with a cup of coffee in his hand, the papers under his arm, when McMahon went down. The old man was an early riser. He had said the first Mass. The smell of coffee carried through the house, coffee and burnt bacon. The monsignor stopped at the office door and looked back at him. "Don't you want the papers?"

"Not till later, thank you."

"You spent the ten by the looks of you."

"Most of it."

"Did you have a good time at least?"

He thought of the youngsters and the fire truck, and the beads now lying on his bedside table like a rosary. "A fine time," he said. Then, remembering Phelan: "How did I make *The Times?*"

"Finding the victim."

"Ah, of course." He cleared his throat.

"You'll be in fine voice for the nuptial Mass," the old man said dryly.

McMahon had forgotten the wedding, and he had promised a final rehearsal after the eight o'clock Mass. At ten there was a funeral which Purdy would take. He was fonder of funerals than he was of weddings. But so was McMahon, to admit the truth. Or would have been that morning.

"They'll give us a good lunch at Costello's after the reception," the old man said. "But I hope to God they serve French champagne. The sweet stuff turns my stomach."

McMahon went out the side door and across the cement yard to the sacristy. He knelt on the prie-dieux near the sanctuary while Father Gonzales finished the seven-thirty Mass, which was in Spanish. Suppose it had been Gonzales whom Carlos had run into? Gonzales who knew nothing of Mrs. Phelan and her marital problems, whom Brogan would never have asked to go on the town with him. Or even going, Gonzales might not have been able to identify Phelan even if he wanted to. It was that which stuck in his craw. But there were more things than that in his craw. If it had not been Muller it would have been something else. What is it about, Lord? I shall try to be silent and hear.

He said his own Mass with no more than twenty or thirty people in the church, and most of them there for the wedding rehearsal. The lector read in Spanish and in English. When the priest raised his hand in the final blessing, he noticed the girl rise and leave the church by the side door. He noticed her because she left without genuflecting. He spoke to the wedding party from the altar to say he would be out in a few minutes.

He was removing the chasuble when the girl he had seen leave the church came into the sacristy. She was tall and quite thin, with heavy black hair down to her shoulders and large dark eyes.

"Excuse me, sir. Are you Father McMahon?"

"I am."

The eyes were not furtive, but she was uneasy. "Am I not allowed to come in here?" she said.

"Why not?" And trying to put her at ease, "We've no secrets."

A little smile. She wore no makeup. But she was not as young as he had thought at first.

He waited before removing the white alb. "Do you want to talk? I'm afraid I have a wedding party out there for a practice run, but it won't take long."

"I'll go," she said, and put out her hand as though to guide her turn back to the door. Then she shoved the hand into the pocket of her skirt. "Just tell me, what was he like, the man you found?"

"Are you Mim?"

Her head shot up, the lips parted and the eyes grew even wider than before. The face froze in his memory, for almost the instant he said the name she whirled around and was gone. He went to the door after her and called out. But she was running between the sunlight and shadow down the long passageway with all her might. He went out, vestments and all, but by the time he reached the street she was nowhere in sight. The restless groom was pacing the church steps. McMahon did not question him, and he conducted the rehearsal as he was, the white alb billowing out as he strode up and down the aisle.

* * *

The visitation haunted him all day, the face as vivid as a Rouault saint—if Rouault had ever painted saints. Between the funeral and wedding Masses, he went to see Mrs. Morales and explained to her and the other women on the stoop that the funeral arrangement was not possible.

The women talked among themselves in Spanish too rapid for his limping understanding of it. Mrs. Morales conducted the council with her hairbrush with which she had been grooming her older daugher's hair. Anita translated for him: "My mother will bake the cake and put out candles, Father. She wants to know, will you come tonight and say the prayers for the dead?"

"After nine," he said. "After confessions."

A woman in curlers—he remembered her from the stoop the day before—gave a toss of her head to the apartment windows alongside. "Father, he's back."

He knew she referred to Phelan, but why tell him? It was the same woman who had suggested to him that Carlos' mother was not home very often. A purveyor of mischief, Mrs. Vargas, no doubt.

"Good," he said and left quickly.

After the wedding Mass—he excused himself from the luncheon—he spent a half hour on the next month's calendar of parish activities, then an hour on music, feeling all the while that it should have been the other way around. Then having a few minutes before religious instruction, he took the musical score to *The Bells* into the choir loft and tried it on the pipe organ. The old church fairly vibrated. He pulled out stops that set free voices in the organ that might never have been sounded before in all its years of muted trebling beneath a spinster's hands. Then to the instructions: for baptized Protestants entering matrimony with Catholics, eager promises and runaway eyes. It was like stamping passports and letting the luggage go. On the subject of birth control, Father? No problem at all to celibates: the words went through his head even as he repeated the church doctrine as lately redefined by the Holy Father.

Miss Lalor made him a special tea and brought it up to

his room on a tray, little sandwiches made up of the fish left from the supper he had not come home to the night before, and the pudding from lunch, but with fresh custard, all done daintily. The thing he was forever forgetting about Miss Lalor was that after her tempers, if you didn't appease them, she came round on a courtship of her own.

"I sent your other suit to the cleaners, Father. You got something muckety on it."

"Thank you."

"It struck me afterwards, if you'd wore it yesterday maybe you were saving it for the police?"

"No."

She lingered in the doorway, wanting to talk about the murder, but unsure of a safe way in. "Wasn't it nice, them mentioning in the papers that you're the director of the Girls' Choir?"

"Nice?" he said, scowling.

"I suppose you're right. There isn't anything they wouldn't turn to publicity nowadays. Eat something, Father. You're losing too much weight."

He said nothing, wanting her squat, corseted, lavender-scented presence removed from his doorway.

"Do you want the door closed, Father?"

"Please."

Alone, he conjured again the girl's face. He was trying, he told himself, to compare it with his memory of the dead man's, and there was not any comparison to be made except in his own sense of bereavement at losing both of them so soon. In all the city, and she had fled into the heart of Manhattan, where would you go to look for a dark-haired, dark-eyed girl named Mim? The Duminy Bar? He had thought of going there, but that was Priscilla Phelan's territory and he did not want to tread on that. Besides, if the girl had known him there, she would not have needed to come to McMahon to inquire what the dead man looked like. She had lost track of him and she had known him by another name, McMahon felt sure. Muller—Mahler: was that the association that had brought her? He felt no incumbence to go to the police. She had not identified the victim, only to herself. Of one thing he was sure: he would not again be used as Brogan had used him, and if he never saw Brogan again, so much the better.

A half hour later he went back to see Rosenberg. The pawnbroker was glad to see him, but he shook his head. "Ach, Father, for me writing is like trying to take fleas from a dog. As soon as I think I have one it disappears into another part of the anatomy. But I will keep trying."

"Perhaps we should talk," McMahon said.

"Nothing would give me more pleasure, but on Saturday afternoon I am busy like no other day in the week. You know how the old song goes. Nobody who can raise a buck wants to be broke on Saturday night."

Even as he spoke a well-dressed young man came into the shop, removing and winding his watch. Rosenberg asked the priest to wait. McMahon watched the transaction from the back of the shop, the gestures, the expressions. He did not hear the words, but the ceremony was as ancient as the charge of usury against the Jews. Another customer came in, this one in a Mexican serape. He reclaimed his guitar with a kind of shamefaced emotion, like someone getting his brother out of jail. Rosenberg, before handing it over to the boy, ran his own fingers over the strings. You see, he seemed to be saying, it had been in good hands.

He came back and entered both transactions in his ledger. He took off his glasses.

"Just one question today," McMahon said. "Did he ever speak of a girl, Mim, Min, something like that?"

"Many girls but not often by name. Nana Marie. I remember that one. I liked that name, Nana Marie."

Nim for short, McMahon thought. He wanted to be careful not to start the old man's thoughts in flight from whatever his association might be. It was a pleasant memory, whatever it was. Then very quietly the priest started: "Where were they together? What kind of neighborhood—or what were they doing?"

"Making love, I should think. Excuse me, Father."

"I'd think so too," he encouraged, "but where?"

"There would be a Greek church and it would be a poor neighborhood, for he loved poverty as much as honor. To him poverty was the only honor. No, that is not right. It is the climate of honor. God protect me! If only I could write it down and get it straight." He struck his temples with his fists.

"It will come, my friend. It will come. Perhaps we can help one another."

"I will not do this for the police, Father. Honor will not be confused with justice, not by Abel Rosenberg. Where in this world is justice, will you tell me that? And if there is a world in which there is justice, tell me why there is none in this? God is just, you will say, and I will say that is because man is not."

McMahon smiled. "I have said nothing, my friend. If I had, I'd have said, God is merciful, and that would have upset you even more."

"Pah! Mercy. Excuse me again. But it was the police who spoke of justice. They were here. I told them about the books. Now they will check the stores for their inventories. Let them. Nothing will be missing except the man himself."

"The Greek church," McMahon prompted gently.

"Very old—in a forgotten place, forgotten people: he said that. Beautiful old . . ." He made an elongated shape with his hands.

"Icons?" McMahon suggested.

He shook his head. "The delicate chains from the rafters to hold the candle bowls, beautiful in the dark of night. He was a janitor. There's an old-fashioned word for you, a janitor. He would not call himself a building superintendent, not my friend Gust."

"Not a man to pretend to greatness," McMahon said.

"It is so, and it was to not pretend to anything, that was how he wanted to live."

"You wonder what his talent was like," the priest mused. "I have a feeling it was valuable."

"Beware of feelings, Father. They are the biggest liars in us. They make truth what we want it to be." He looked to the front of the shop as the door opened again, and flung his hands in a gesture of hopelessness. "Look what this one is bringing me. An accordion. He will want a fortune for it, ivory and mother-of-pearl. And if he cannot redeem it, where will I find a street singer?"

McMahon said, "I must go. There will be a memorial tonight in the building where he lived. No funeral until the police are good and ready. I've promised to say a few prayers. You would be welcome, Mr. Rosenberg." He wrote the address on a card the pawnbroker gave him.

"Will you play Bach and Mahler?"

"If there's anything to play it on, I might."

"He would like it better than the prayers. And to tell you the truth, Father, I would too."

But Rosenberg did not go to the Morales apartment, and Father McMahon did not play Bach or Mahler. A visit to the stoop of 987 in the daytime was quite different from going up those steps at nine-thirty on a warm Saturday night. The sound of an electric guitar twanged through the building, and somewhere a Calypso singer was tuned in at top volume, and above it all, a cacophony of voices, one pitched higher than another.

A dim light shone in the windows of the Phelan apartment, but there was no light at all in the vestibule. He had to follow the voices. The ceiling bulbs in the hallway were caged in wire mesh. He began a slow, reluctant ascent. The smell of disinfectant was so strong it hurt his nostrils, yet it could not quite kill the undersmell of the communal bathroom on each floor. Behind a closed door a child was crying. He could just hear it through the raucous din, the loneliest of sounds, and one that angered him. A gang of teenagers thundered down the steps. He backed against the wall to let them pass, the girls rattling and sparkling with cheap jewelry, scented with heavy perfume, the boys with glossy hair and clattering, highly shined boots. He recognized Anita and called out after her.

"Upstairs, Father. Everybody."

On the second flight of stairs a fat grandmother was lumbering up, one painful step at a time, and at every pause she shouted a gutter invective, not for what was going on, but because it was going on without her.

A man leaned over the banister and baited her.

"Bastard!" She shook her fist at him.

He and another came down the steps and between them hauled her up. On the last step he groped her fat buttocks and goosed her. She shrieked and swung her arm around on him, almost tumbling them all down the stairs.

And among these people in so short a time, McMahon thought, Muller had found a welcome. He was far less confident of his own and he had been in the parish for eleven years.

But the women made way for him, pushing their men to the side, black men and brown and sallow-white, almost as varied as the colors of their shirts. Mrs. Morales shouted the two crowded rooms into silence. Someone turned off the record player, the last few notes wilting away. The guitarist was in another part of the building and someone closed the door on him. It helped a little. As Mrs. Morales led McMahon toward the inner room, he noticed Dan Phelan sitting in a corner, a glass in both hands, his eyes on the glass and his face as taut as the fingers around the glass. His wife sat on the arm of his chair. She was made up with her old flair, defiance in every feature.

A sideboard was spread with food in the second room, but it was not toward it that Carlos' mother drew him. It was toward a small round table where a candle burned alongside a shoebox. A chill ran down the priest's back when he saw what was in the box: a waxen colored doll laid out as in a coffin, a doll clothed as a man and made from child to man by the crude gluing on of a black beard. When his first shock was spent, McMahon realized that it was probably Anita who had given a swatch of her hair to the making of the beard. The unpliable hands of the doll were crossed over a bunch of violets.

Out of the corner of his eye the priest saw Mrs. Morales make the sign of the cross and he sensed rather than saw the others who had pressed into the room after him do the same. He lifted his eyes to the picture which hung on the wall behind the table, the placid, bearded, long-haired Christ with his forefinger touching the flaming heart. It was a picture familiar to him from childhood on, but in that instant, as alien as the shrouded doll.

He bent his head and prayed silently, but for himself.

The people were waiting to hear his words, but when, after a moment, he raised his head, they assumed his silent prayer appropriate and said their amens.

"You like it, Father, *si?*" Mrs. Morales said of the boxed figure, her gold teeth shining as she smiled.

"Beautiful," he said, and turned away determined not to look again at the picture of the Sacred Heart. Yet the words ran through his mind: Most Sacred Heart of Jesus, I place my trust in thee.

"Please, Father, take something to eat. The stuffed crabs I make myself."

"Have a drink, Father. We brought the whisky, and I'll have one with you." It was Phelan who spoke, having come up beside him, bottle in hand. He had a deep voice for so slight a man. McMahon tried to suppress the thought, but it came again, the wife's telling, 'Like a bull, Father.'

"Thank you," McMahon said. "I will have a drink."

Mrs. Morales gave him a glass, wiping it first with her apron.

When he held out his glass, two of the younger men present held theirs out to Phelan, too, and Pedrito Morales came up with his. Phelan poured without a word, generously, but with his lips clamped tight. He quarter-filled his own glass before setting the bottle on the table. Everyone held his glass, waiting. McMahon finally lifted his toward the effigy and said, "Peace be with him."

The men all drank. Pedrito coughed and wiped his mouth on his sleeve. "Irish piss," he said.

Phelan threw the contents of his glass in the boy's face. It all happened with flashing instancy: Pedrito flung his own glass over his shoulder and started for Phelan; Phelan, with one step backward, drew a knife from his pocket and switched the blade. McMahon was a few seconds reacting, for the last person in the room he expected to carry a knife was Phelan. He leaped between the men and ordered Phelan in the name of God to put it away. Phelan stood his ground and made jerky little stabs with the knife, trying to motion the priest out of his way. Behind McMahon, the men were derisive, their mockery the filth of two languages, and the women more contemptuous than the men.

Priscilla Phelan came up behind her husband and locked her arms around his neck, pulling his head back. McMahon caught his arm and twisted it until he let go the knife. The priest put his foot on the blade. It was not necessary. No one wanted it. Muller had been killed with a knife. McMahon picked it up, flicked the blade closed and put the knife in his own pocket.

Phelan had gone limp. He stood in a slouch, his eyes wild with hatred. His wife gave him a push toward the door. He pulled himself up straight then and walked with the controlled, exaggerated dignity of the drunk which McMahon knew well. At the door he spat and went out.

Priscilla Phelan tossed her red hair back over her shoulders. "This is my house, you bastards! You tell the police about this and out you go, every mother-selling one of you."

Mrs. Morales was scolding the instigators, the rilers among the crowd. The fat grandmother sat and rocked herself with pleasure. She clapped her hands. McMahon kept catching flashes of faces, of gestures, bare arms and laughing mouths, a girl draped over a chair, her legs fanning the air. And noise, noise, noise. Mrs. Phelan went out, her hips swaggering, and the men whistled and hooted, and one of them pranced a few steps as if to follow, stopped, and gave a roundhouse sweep of his arm, his thumb in the air. The

Calypso music went on again. It was all over. And it wasn't that the party resumed, the explosion was part of the party, the language a kind of vernacular, and the noise was a way of life. No one apologized to the priest. Someone brought him his drink where he had put it down on the table when Phelan drew the knife. Mrs. Morales brought him a plate with two stuffed crabs and some pastries.

"Where is Carlos?" he asked her.

"In bed," she said. She indicated the door to a room off the parlor.

The boy could not have slept through that noise. "May I look in on him?"

She shrugged. It was up to him.

McMahon ate a few bites of the food and went to the bedroom door. He opened it, expecting to see the youngster wide-eyed and staring out at him as when he and Brogan had found him in the hut. Instead, he saw four bundled shapes beneath a blanket, children huddled together like puppies in a box, and all of them sound asleep.

The door to the Phelan apartment was open when he went down the stairs a few minutes later. She would be watching for him, and in any case, he wanted to get rid of the knife in his pocket. She called out to him to come in and then closed the door behind him.

Phelan stood, his back to them, and stared out the window. There was an Irish look to the apartment, which was merely to say McMahon felt a familiarity there not present for him in the rest of the building: it was the curtains, perhaps, just the curtains that made the difference, full, window-length, and white.

McMahon laid the knife on the side table on top of a copy of the *Daily News*.

"Dan's in real trouble now, Father. The police picked him up in a bar last night, and he can't even remember where he'd been in the morning."

He could remember, McMahon thought, but he was not telling. Protecting a man, perhaps. The police would have suspected that, picking him up where they had. He pointed to the knife. "Where did that come from?"

"It's been in the house for years," she said. "But why in the name of God he had to take it up there with him tonight, I don't know."

Phelan turned from the window. "Don't you, Priscilla? I think you do." He was about to sit down. "Would you like a drink, Father? There's another bottle, I think."

McMahon shook his head. "No, thanks."

Phelan slumped into the chair and shaded his eyes with his hand. A gentle hand, McMahon would have said.

"Do you know what I think, Father?" Mrs. Phelan said. "I think he wants to be charged with the murder. Big shot! He wants to be a big shot to a houseful of freaks."

Phelan was shaking his head.

McMahon thought: it's being a freak in a houseful of big shots that's killing the man. He sat down on the couch near Phelan. "If I spoke to a doctor, Dan, would you go and see him?"

Phelan took his hand away from his eyes. A sad smile twisted at the corners of his mouth. "A psychiatrist?"

"Yes."

"He doesn't need a doctor. I told you that yesterday, Father. He's all right now."

Phelan looked from one to the other of them, and then at his own hands which he put palms together, the shape of prayer. No man ever showed more eloquently his sense of betrayal. McMahon got up. Twice, by inadvertence—or by some destiny that was tracking himself as well—McMahon had betrayed him. "Come and see me if you want to, Dan. Or call the rectory and we can meet somewhere else."

"In the jail maybe," his wife said, "if he keeps this up."

McMahon said nothing until she had followed him into the hallway. "Do you want to kill him or save him? I don't want the answer, but you'd better find it for yourself, Mrs. Phelan."

"Father . . ." She put her hands to her ears.

The electric guitar, the Calypso singer, and now someone on the drums.

"All I want is peace. Really, that's all I want."

"We could all say the same thing," McMahon said. "But where is it?"

"Thank you, Father," she said after him as he went down the steps.

For what? But he nodded and went on. A priest expected thanks, always thanks and only thanks, and a glass of whisky on the house. He was about to cross the street mid-block when he heard her scream, and he knew what it was the instant he heard it, and he felt that somewhere in his soul he had expected that also. After all, he had given the man back the knife. He ran the half block to the police call box where he had reported the death of Muller.

8

Phelan had botched his attempted suicide. He might die of the wound he had attempted to inflict on his own heart, but not if the surgical team at St. Jude's hospital could prevent it. He was in surgery for three hours, a nightmare of time McMahon spent with Mrs. Phelan and the police, one of whom called the priest's attention to the fact that for Muller to have lived long enough to talk with him, that job also had been botched. The consensus seemed to be — although no one said so in so many words — Phelan did not know much about anatomy. Then, to make matters worse, sitting in the small office provided by the night supervisor, Priscilla Phelan broke down and confessed to the police her affair with Muller.

Traynor said, "So you are unfaithful to him; you were unfaithful to a homosexual."

"He's not."

Traynor turned his cold gray eyes on McMahon. "Father?"

"I have nothing to say." Then: "Mrs. Phelan ought to know she has right of counsel before talking to you."

"I'm sure she was so informed," Traynor said with the quiet sarcasm that was always in his voice. He turned to the detective who had answered the first call. "Tonelli?"

"Yes, sir. I told her that."

Priscilla Phelan's eyes darted from one to the other of the detectives. "What are you trying to say to me?"

"You didn't know *that* about your husband?" Traynor said.

McMahon intervened. "Do you know it for a fact, lieutenant? Or do you know only that the man was picked up in a bar frequented by homosexuals?"

"You will make an excellent witness, Father. Or even counsel, you seem so well equipped."

Mrs. Phelan pounded her fists on her knees. "Give it to me straight, officer. What is it you're trying to tell me about Dan?"

"Father McMahon has pointed out the inadmissibility of hearsay—that's a nice word for it—hearsay on the street, in your home building, in the bar in question—hearsay. So all I can do for you, Mrs. Phelan, is ask a question. Without a lawyer, you don't need to answer it. You were unfaithful to your husband: did he attack *you* for it?"

"He screwed me!" she shouted. "Yes, you bastards, so don't try to give me that fag crap about Dan. Now get out of here and leave me alone."

"I wish we could do that, but we can't. We all have to wait—except Father, if he wishes to go—but we can pray the man lives to speak for himself." Traynor stretched his legs, put his hands behind his head and closed his eyes.

McMahon stayed. Three hours in hell. The detectives smoked, Priscilla Phelan chain-smoked. The detectives talked about their families, about baseball, about war and draft dodgers, about the kids today, and their own kids, most of them ashamed to say their father was a cop. My old man was a cop and I was proud of it. Dropouts and freakouts, but nobody mentioned fallouts. Then word came that Phelan had been taken to the intensive-care ward. There was a good chance that he would live. The detectives matched coins to see which of them would take the first four-hour shift at his bedside.

McMahon went as far as the ward door with Mrs. Phelan. She would be able to look in now and then on the trussed and tubed and taped figure of the man who had not been allowed to die, and she would take up the vigil meanwhile on the hard bench among the other watchers at the swinging door between life and death. Here was the documentary to the night's violence, and here among the watchers was a brotherhood of man that leapt all barriers, color, language, money. There was but one further reduction to the common denominator of humanity: the dead knew no prejudice.

After baptisms the next day, which was Sunday, Father McMahon commenced his search for the girl who had known Muller. Poverty and an Orthodox church, an old, forgotten church.

On Monday afternoon, having abandoned the classified phone book for an outdated map of the city, and Greek Orthodox for Russian or Ukrainian, he walked down from Tompkins Square to Fifth Street and then east. Poverty was assuredly served by the street market on Avenue B. Used shoes hung on stands in clusters, there were bins of battered pots and patched-up toys. Mickey Mouse T-shirts and lingerie, chipped glassware and gaudy pottery. The vendors looked like gypsies but they spoke a voluble Yiddish, and Spanish if they had to. There were fruit stands and vegetables with Lexington Avenue prices. A woman might haggle the price of a washcloth, but she counted out twelve cents for a pound of potatoes and never said a word. McMahon walked on, his hands in his pockets, his eyes to the windows which always measured a neighborhood for him: the state of the curtains (that Irish core in him again); there were not many curtains at all now, but where there were, there were often window boxes as well, and he could see the red bloom of geraniums stretching their growth toward the sun. He looked in on a youth center: there were more boys on the street than inside, and children clamoring over old cars, spitting the dust and making faces on the windshields. And the flower children were here, bearded and beaded, and baited by the squares. He stopped a girl with an infant strapped on her back and inquired if she knew of a Greek or Russian church nearby.

"I know where there's a synagogue," she said, pointing, "and the mission house on the corner. We've started a nurs-

ery school there. It's cooperative and doesn't cost much—
if you know of anyone who wants to join."

"I'll remember," he said, pleased, in slacks and sweater,
to be taken for a native.

"He won't like it much." She gave a hoist to the child
saddled on her back. "But he'll get used to it. He'll have
to."

McMahon knew by her speech, the modulation of her
voice, that the home she had come from was far from a city
slum.

"He looks pretty sophisticated to me," McMahon said.
And the child did, gazing solemnly around him for something worthy of his attention. That his nose leaked like a
faucet seemed to disturb neither him nor his mother.

The girl, and she was only that, smiled broadly. "Man,
he's so sophisticated he won't even talk."

McMahon thought about that as he walked on, the so-
phistication of not talking. The voice of silence. Something
was happening to him in these hours of search he stole from
the day's routine. He stole them chiefly from music, and
therefore from himself. But walking the streets, he listened
for another music, other sounds, and permitted unfamiliar
thoughts to dangle in his mind: in a way, it was like listening
for the voice of God instead of drowning it out with prayer.
And save for the wine at the altar, he had not had a drink
in two days.

St. Chrysostom Church stood out for him by its very
inconspicuousness. A narrow building of gray stone, it
hunched in the shadows of the soot-blackened fortress which
was a public school built, according to the cornerstone, in
1896. McMahon tried the front door of the church. It was
locked but he could hear voices within. He went to the side
door. The smell of incense, to which he had thought himself
inured, came at him like something alive rushing to get out
the door.

There was no vestibule. The door opened directly into
the church. Several older women and a few men arose from
the benches along the walls just as he entered. The bearded

Orthodox priest, fully robed, came from the sanctuary, censer in hand. He censed first the icons and then, one by one, each man and woman and McMahon too when he reached him. McMahon resisted the impulse to bow low in response as in the solemn high Mass of Rome. The priest moved on to those along the other wall. The church was lighted by small amber-glassed windows near the ceiling, and by the lamps hanging from the rafters on delicately wrought chains of varying lengths. Such had Rosenberg described from his conversations with Muller. The celebrant priest vanished from sight behind the gates of the sanctuary: ecumenism had not yet invaded this shrine of orthodoxy.

McMahon slipped out of the church. He wondered what the occasion was for the afternoon service. How little he knew of any calendar except his own. He had studied Greek in his seminary days, but the smattering of it left to him now was scarcely more than sufficed to tell him that the church inscription was in a different alphabet.

He began looking for "Nana Marie" on the hallway letter boxes of the building on the corner of Avenue A. A forlorn search, for while there were several names on most boxes, they were last names only. Mostly Spanish, some Slovak, one Irish name in the first two buildings. He stopped a square-faced sturdy policewoman, whose white belt and strap proclaimed her special duty at school crossings. She did not know anyone by the name of Nana Marie or Nim. By sight, maybe. She knew almost everyone by sight except the Puerto Ricans. Three quarters of her own people had moved away in the past ten years, respectable people with trades—bakers, upholsterers; her brother was a bricklayer who had moved to Staten Island. "Hunkies," she said with a kind of pride. "That's what they called us in the old days. We didn't like it, but we didn't beat up people for it, and the way this neighborhood used to be, you could eat off the street it was so clean."

While she spoke McMahon saw the girl and recognized her even in the distance, the wide skirt and a jacket open, and an overstuffed bag at her waist, the strap to which she shifted from one shoulder to the other as she came. He liked her walk, the jauntiness of it.

The policewoman, seeing that she had lost his interest, moved on. McMahon called out his thanks but he dared not take his eyes from the girl for fear she might vanish into a building on the way. But she came on, saying a word here and there to the children, to a boy polishing a car. She stopped, turning into the building where McMahon waited on the stoop, with the uncertain look on her face of having seen him somewhere before.

"I'm Joseph McMahon," he said. "Remember?"

She came up the steps. With a sidelong glance and a sly little smile, she said, "Hello, Joe."

She slung the strap from her shoulder, disentangling it from her hair, and gave him the woven bag, taking for granted that he would carry it and follow her into the building. She opened the mailbox marked "Lavery."

"I wondered who the Irishman was in this lot," he said. "Miss or Mrs.?"

"Nim," she said, and took two or three pieces of mail from the box.

"Nana Marie," McMahon said.

"Just Nim." She led him up one flight of dust-encrusted stairs after another. There were books in the bag and what he took to be a drawing pad.

"That's quite a climb," he said, waiting while she put her key in the lock of the front apartment on the top floor.

"Even for the cockroaches," she said.

She opened the door on a room that was as bright as the halls were dingy, one huge room, the walls broken through, but pillars had been left and painted like barber poles. An easel stood alongside the front windows. A floor to ceiling rack contained many canvases standing on their sides. Everything was pin neat, although to be sure, everything was not much.

She took her bag from him and hung it on the back of the door. "Would you care for a drink?"

"No. No thank you. Why did you run away when I asked if you were Nim?"

"Why have you come after me?"

"I wanted to know more," he said.

"About him?"

"Yes."

"Don't you think he'd have told you if he wanted you to know?"

"There wasn't time. He died too soon."

"Everybody does, except those who die too late and they're already dead."

"You're a very judgmental young lady. That's supposed to be my department."

"I guess I am," she said. "I don't have many chairs. That's the comfortable one. Please take it." She motioned him toward a rattan rocker and then took off her jacket and hung it over the bag on the door hook.

He took the moment to look around the room, at the posters, the paintings. But he wanted more to look at her.

"I like the floor myself," she said and sat on a rush mat, folded her legs and spread the wide skirt over them. "What did he tell you about me?"

"That once you said he would shake hands with the devil. Only that."

She leaned her elbows on her knees and her chin on her folded hands. There were marks of trouble or just possibly of dissipation that should not have lined the face of one as young as he thought her to be. The eyes filled with sadness. She tried to throw it off. "Do you think he did? Go like that, I mean: ready for anything—or nothing?"

"Let me tell you what those few minutes were like," McMahon said. "Sometimes I think I dreamt them, they're so vivid, surrealistic in the way things stand out in a dream, the hands, the shadows, the sounds. The smell of the place: all the incense in that church across the street this afternoon won't take the smell of that cellar from my memory. But it was what he said to me that makes connection, Miss Nim, that breaks through the dream. Or maybe strengthens it."

He rocked back in the chair and wondered just for an instant why he felt so right in being in it, in being where he was. Within the compass of his gaze was a painting in grays, browns and ocher, a cubistic city with shapes like half-lidded eyes cornered in the windows. "You're a window-watcher, too," he said and pointed to the picture.

"You don't want to tell me what he said."

"I'm holding back, amn't I? I wonder why. It wasn't so much *what* he had said either, but the sheer bravura of saying it at a time like that. He lived till he died. Do you know what I mean?"

She closed her eyes and nodded vehemently. It was what she had wanted to hear.

"You loved him, didn't you?"

"There hasn't been anyone since, and that's not like me." She gave a dry little laugh. "I wish I had his child, and that's not like me either."

"What is like you?"

She shook her head. "You were going to tell me . . ."

"This?" he said, indicating the room. "I've never gone into a house so clean, so neat."

"That's me on the outside," she said. "Please tell me!"

"I was writing a sermon," he said. "That's how it begins and I've got to tell it that way, because he asked me what I was doing when the youngster came for me."

"You were writing a sermon. What about? He'd want to know that too."

"Brotherhood," he said defensively, feeling that she also would have little affinity with sermons.

Her smile was flashing, brief. "I'm sorry."

"That's what religion is about," McMahon said, even more defensively.

"I'd like to think so." She drew a quick, deep breath. "Father McMahon was writing a sermon, and my poor runaway lover was dying in a stinking cellar."

He told her then, re-creating the scene down to the small-est detail he could remember, from the words on the sidewalk to the way the man had turned his head in on himself to die.

At that picture, she covered her face and wept, letting the sobs come out as they would. McMahon got up and went to the east windows, avoiding the easel where it stood by the windows overlooking the church, roughly north. He walked softly on the bare red-painted floor. He could see the river, a barge coming into view as it passed the new housing complex between Avenue A and the Drive. On the tarred rooftop two stories below him were old whisky bottles, beer cans, and things he recognized as contraceptives just before she spoke.

"Don't look down," she said. "In this part of the city, we always look up. That's where the sky is."

"A little bit of heaven," he murmured, turning back to her.

She blew her nose violently. "What?"

"That's one of the monsignor's favorite songs. A non sequitur, but it ran through my mind. I'll explain." He found himself then telling her in almost a stream of consciousness about his parish life, then about the tenement where Muller had lived and the Phelans, not about Mrs. Phelan's confidences of course, but of the police inquisition and then at the end, because it relieved him to tell it, of the way he had betrayed Phelan, identifying him in the Village bar.

"A homosexual bar?" Her intuition was quick. Or perhaps it was his own naïveté.

"Yes." He went on to describe the memorial in the Morales apartment and its aftermath.

She was sitting on the floor still, but now with one arm propped on the daybed so that he saw her face in profile, the long straight nose, the strong chin. "Do you know what I think, Joe—I can't call you 'Father.' You don't mind, do you?"

"Please. I like to hear the name once in a while. The monsignor calls me Joseph. Otherwise . . . please do. What is it that you think?"

She sighed and then said it: "My boy was sleeping with the Phelan woman."

McMahon did not say anything, and he looked quickly away when she surprised him with a flashing glance to his face.

"A man's got to sleep with someone . . . I guess. And he wasn't coming back." She got up and paced the room, almost boyish, her pacing, and yet she was very feminine.

"You're sure of that?"

"Oh, yes. That's one thing I've learned: no marriage band, they don't come back. Not that a marriage band brings them back either. I didn't try to look for him. I tried to forget him until I read in the paper about your finding a man named Gustave Muller."

"Mahler?" McMahon said.

"Exactly. *The Song of Earth.* I've got his records. You talk about the monsignor and his sentimental songs. Do you smoke?"

He shook his head.

She went to her jacket pocket and got a cigarette. He thought of taking the match from her and lighting the cigarette, but he didn't do it. She lit it herself and then inhaled deeply before going on. "Dark and velvet-toned: me and Kathleen Ferrier." She laughed self-consciously, having said it.

Again McMahon was tempted, this time to say that it was so. He said nothing.

"Gustave Muller. It sounds like a house painter, doesn't it? Do you know what he did for a buck here?"

"Janitor for the church. For how much? Ten dollars a week?"

"Twelve. We got along. I have a job from twelve to four. I'm a pretty good secretary. Forty dollars a week, take home twenty-five. Taxes, old-age security. Security—it's nice to think it can come out of a paycheck." She glanced at him. "But then you've got it made, haven't you? How did you know about the janitor work?" She spoke rapidly, nervously, as though she was afraid to stay on any one subject for very long.

"A man named Rosenberg: I got three things from him, janitor, the Orthodox Church and Nana Marie. He was a friend to whom Muller talked a great deal, a pawnbroker on Ninth Avenue. Nim, you said you didn't try to find him. I think somebody did. I don't think Phelan killed him. I feel as sure of that—a lot more sure than I am of salvation. My word for security."

"I like it better. I hate security."

Because you haven't got it, McMahon thought, no more than I salvation. "What I'm trying to say is, I think somebody he didn't expect to find him, did. He knew the man. That much I'm sure of."

"I know what you're saying. I don't care."

"That's remarkable, if you mean it. He did not care either. There's a philosophy at work here that I don't understand."

"If he had his reasons for not telling you, they're enough for me," she said. "I didn't know him by the name Muller. It was just the feeling, and pure accident I picked up *The Times* at the office that day. I didn't know his real name either. That was part of the way he chose to search himself— for himself. He wasn't afraid of much. I have a lot of fears, but he didn't. The only thing he was afraid of was becoming somebody that somebody else thought he ought to be. I've never seen his painting, do you know? And we lived together for over a year. But whatever's good in my work, and I'm beginning to believe in it myself, is what he taught me. There's a time to lie fallow, he would say. Come fallow with me. His puns were awful."

McMahon wished she would slow down for a moment. He wanted to think about the phrase, becoming somebody that other people thought he ought to be. But she went on.

"Do you know how I met him? I was working in a gallery then on Tenth Street—secretary, messenger, a lot of things. Anyway, he came in out of the rain one night and I was there alone. It was a perfectly terrible night, the weather I mean. He crawled out from under what looked like a tar-

paulin and dropped it by the door. He went from one painting
to another—the artist is pretty bad, I think, but he's got a
Madison Avenue gallery now—and he didn't say a word
until he had looked at them all. The artist's name—well,
I'll tell you, it's Kenyon, but he signs his things just with
the letter K. Finally Stu said: 'K presumably knows K in-
timately. I know a painter who signs himself E—E for Ego,
but for the opposite reason. Or is K for Kokomo?'" Nim
reminded McMahon of the member of the monkey family
written up for his art work.

"'I'll tell Mr. K you recognized his style.' I said, something like that. He looked at me in that very intense way
of his—like the person was a painting too. 'And who are
you?'" She mimicked a slightly clipped speech. "I'd had it
for the day, I'd almost had it for life at that period. 'I'm an
aging hippie,' I said. 'Well, since I'm a dirty old man, let's
close up this zoo and have coffee together.' We did and I
talked a lot, mostly about me, and afterwards he walked
me home here under that crazy tarpaulin of his and I remembered he did smell like a dirty old man, but I guess
Sir Walter Raleigh did too, and I liked him quite a lot. I
ought to say—maybe it doesn't matter—but before we left
the gallery I asked him to sign the visitor's book, just to
prove I'd been there after the boss went home. He thought
about it for a couple of minutes before he signed. I think
he was making up a name then, Stuart Robinson. I said I'd
call him Stu, and he said it was appropriate since he was a
reformed drunk, a member of AAA." She smiled wryly,
remembering.

"I said, 'AA, you mean.' And he said, 'No, Alcoholics
Anonymous Anonymous....' And another time, I asked him
what his own painting was like. Another of his lousy puns:
Anonymous Bosch." She pulled hard at her cigarette and
sent the smoke to the ceiling. "Bosch and Tchelitchew. He
said that was how nature hung him up too. He didn't like
nature. The outdoors, I mean, trees and sky and water. They
hurt too much."

McMahon thought of telling her about the art books,

including Bosch, at Rosenberg's, but it would wait. He said: "When did he go away from here, Nim?"

"Sixty-three days before the day he died. How's that for remembering?"

"It's been easier," the priest said, "than it's going to be to forget."

She made a noise of ironic agreement. "Are you sure about that drink?"

"For now I am." He wanted to think about her and Muller.

She squashed the cigarette out in the tray at her feet, grinding the butt into shreds. "Why don't you ask me?"

"Why he left? I assume you would tell me if you wanted me to know."

"It's funny. I said something like that to you in the beginning. Didn't I? And if you'd asked me, I was going to say I thought it was because he was ready to start painting again, and he had to find that place for himself, where he could be the self he was looking for. But I'm not sure of that any more. He didn't say anything. He just went out one day with some of his books and he didn't come back. And that's what I told myself was the reason. But the real reason—I think now—I'm a very conventional person underneath. I wanted something conventional of him."

"Marriage?"

She shrugged. Daylight was beginning to fade. Her face was shadowed. "Security."

"I thought you said you hated security," McMahon said gently.

"I do. But that doesn't make me not want it."

He laughed. "I will have that drink you offered me."

"It's gin."

"I can take it."

She poured two glasses of gin over ice in the kitchen, McMahon watching from the doorway, and told of how Stu had taken out the walls and reinforced the beams with sewer-pipe rejects. McMahon rapped his knuckles against the striped pillars, and the sound was hollow. He told her of Carlos' hut and the doorknobs. They touched their glasses and drank to him.

"Whoever," Nim said.

On the second drink, McMahon proposed the toast, "To life."

"It's what we have, isn't it?" Nim said. "Will you have supper with me? I can make it stretch. You know, instead of hamburger, spaghetti."

He would have liked to stay, for he could feel the ache of her loneliness. Which must be his own, he thought. One does not feel another's pain that keenly. But he declined. "We have a tyrannous housekeeper, and I have work I must do tonight."

"Your father's business—isn't that what the boy Christ said when they found him in the temple?"

"Something like that," McMahon said.

"I don't think I've ever known a priest before, not to talk to like this."

"Not many people do," he said, which was his own truth at least. At the door, having thanked her, he said: "Nim, you could be wrong in why he left."

"I know. It's my way of beating myself, to think it."

"Then stop it, because I think you were right the first time. What we've got to do is find his painting."

Her eyes went moist as she thought about it. "It would almost be like finding his child—in me I mean, and that would be a miracle."

"I believe in them," McMahon said. "And I am convinced, he was not an anonymous man."

"Neither are you,' she said.

Which meant, he supposed, going down the stairs, that to her all priests were just that. And if that had not been what she meant, he did not want to think about it.

9

"The signs are all go, Father," the desk nurse said sportingly. "Except that he can't talk. Or won't. The detectives, I suppose. I shouldn't say that. I don't really know."

"Do they question him?"

"Not that I know of. They just sit and take up space. So does he, Father. We need that bed for people who are dying in the wards because they can't get the care we could give them."

McMahon went into the ward, making his way around beds that could launch into space, so elaborate and delicate their equipment. On each of them lay miraculously live testimony to man's violence on the ground, especially when he used the automobile like a weapon.

Priscilla Phelan was standing at her husband's side, her hand on his taped wrist. A chair had been squeezed in the corner for the plainclothesman. A big man, he was doing his best to keep out of the way: the detail was not one of his own choice.

"It's Father McMahon," Mrs. Phelan said, bending close to her husband's ear.

He did not open his eyes.

The nurse had been right: he had better color than his wife, McMahon thought. It was a good face. There was even strength in the mouth, something the haunted eyes distracted from when you confronted him face on. Mrs. Phelan brushed the hair back from his forehead. She made a gesture of hopelessness to McMahon.

He spoke to the officer. "I'll be responsible while I'm here, detective."

"Okay, Father. I'll have a smoke."

"I will too," the wife said. "Danny, I'll be right outside. Or maybe I'll go home for a little while. I won't be long."

There was no response from Phelan.

McMahon waited, saying nothing, watching the face gradually, almost imperceptibly relax when the silence told him his constant companions were gone. He opened his eyes, screwed them up against the shock of light and then looked at the priest.

"I wish she would never come back," he said.

"She will—until you make yourself better. You're like her child right now." Fleetingly he thought of Nim and her wish for Muller's child.

"That's what I've been for a long time, except..."

"I know."

"Do you? Yes, I remember now."

So did McMahon, the palmed hands, the portrait of betrayal. "Why don't you talk to the police and get them off your back?"

"You too, Father?"

"All right, Dan."

"I wish they'd go away."

"They're gone for now. Did you know him at all, the man Muller?"

"Just as the man in the back room. I didn't want to know him."

"Why?"

"I liked him, that's why. Christ almighty, leave me alone." Phelan tried to fling out the arm with the intravenal tube attached to it. The overhead bottle rocked in its cradle.

McMahon steadied it. "Easy, Dan, easy. I want to help you if I can, not torment you. You see, I don't believe for a minute you could use that knife on anybody but yourself. But let's get off the subject. Do you still want to die?"

"No. But I don't want to live much either."

"There's a difference, a marvelous difference. What would make you want to live?"

Phelan thought about it, his eyes almost closed. Mc-Mahon was afraid for a minute that he had turned off again. But the V deepened between his eyebrows. "If I could be like him."

"In what way?"

"Just in the way he had with people. And I don't mean my wife. The kids, you know . . . just the way he was with them. I can't explain it."

"I know what you mean. I felt that quality in him even in the last minutes of his life. We'll talk tomorrow if you want to, but only if you want to."

"I guess I do. This is kind of wild, Father, when you think about some things, but there was a . . . a holiness about him. Crazy?" He looked up at the priest: a little zeal came into the hitherto fugitive eyes.

McMahon said: "You're an idealist, Dan, and there aren't many left. I want you to live."

"So do the cops, but that's not what they call me."

McMahon leaned close to him. "Screw the cops," he said under his breath.

Phelan parted his teeth in a soundless, almost motionless laugh, and McMahon thanked God for it.

He patted Phelan's shoulder. "Get out of this ward. They need the bed for things you wouldn't believe are human, the way they come in."

"I know. I hear them all night long."

"Tomorrow, Dan."

In the hallway Brogan was waiting with the other detective and a third who was about to relieve his colleague at the bedside. It was the first time McMahon and Brogan had met since their night on the town.

Brogan offered his hand. "A lot of water under the bridge, eh, Father?"

"A lot."

"He talked to you, didn't he? I'm not asking what he said, Father. I mean he can talk if he wants to."

"He can talk."

"But will he? That's the question. Don't worry, Father. I'll wait him out. Got time for coffee?"

"I don't actually. I've got to make the rounds while I'm here." He had taken over from Father Gonzales in this, and Gonzales would take his church history class that afternoon. He had fallen behind in his work with the chorus and the recital was a week off.

Brogan walked down the hall with him. "I was going over your statement again, that crazy conversation with Muller? And you know what I think, Father? That part about taking the knife away from his killer—that could be pure Freud."

"I suppose it could," McMahon said with heavy solemnity.

"I made the mistake of trying it on Traynor. Oh, man. You know what they're calling me now at the station house?"

"Doctor Freud."

"I still think I've got something." He jerked his head in the direction of the ward. "Why won't he talk to us? You don't spend twelve hours sleeping off a drunk someplace you can't even find the next day. No, sir. When you wake up after a night out, you know where you are. Ask me."

McMahon had no such intention. "Brogan, I agree. The man who wants to go home can generally find his way there. And the man who doesn't want to go home needs help. That's where I'd call on Doctor Freud if I were you."

"Me?" Brogan said.

"I wasn't thinking of you. That's your connection." McMahon walked on down the corridor.

He had scheduled an extra hour with the girls' chorus after school that afternoon. He was now wishing that he had chosen a less ambitious program. *The Bells* just weren't swinging: because he wasn't, he knew that, and for that reason, he tried to be more patient than usual with the girls. It crossed his mind that Sister Justine could do as well with them as he was doing, and her programming would be more

to the monsignor's liking, and more to the tastes of most
of his audience. *His* audience. His audience was not the
majority. His was an audience of one, himself. That bit of
self-scrutiny out of the way, he went after the beat he wanted.
He illustrated at the piano, going through the crescendo
passage, accenting with his own baritone voice the pre-
ciseness, the mounting excitement he wanted.

"You've seen it in the movies, on television," he said,
getting up from the piano. "The pioneers trapped in the
stockade, the Indians creeping up on them, closer and closer,
and then *Voom!* the soldiers, the United States cavalry racing
to the rescue. Now, sopranos, you're the pioneers, you're
scared, you feel it in the scalp of your head. Every note is
a cry for help, urgent, more urgent. Mezzos, you're the
Indians. You move in softly, carefully, but you keep coming
on. These people have taken your land, your buffalo, your
way of life. And nobody, but nobody has to tell the United
States cavalry what to do." He motioned Sister Justine back
to the piano and murmured, "May Rachmaninoff lie quiet
in his grave."

After conducting the passage once from the podium,
he went down the steps and up the raked aisle to hear
what it sounded like from the back of the auditorium.
There in the last row, flashing a broad smile, was Nim
Lavery. After the surprise of seeing her, he was both
pleased and angry. The anger was a throwback. He would
have spent it in sarcasm on any other intruder.

She sensed this instantly. "I'm sorry. One of the sisters
brought me here."

"The sisters," he said, rather enjoying Nim's discomfi-
ture, "are not in charge of the choir." He turned back to the
stage. "All right, take it from the beginning."

"I'll wait outside for you," Nim said, about to get up.

"No. It's too late to leave the stockade now." He sat
down beside her, slouched in the seat and closed his eyes,
trying to concentrate on the music. The girls, bless them,
were good. They rose to an audience of more than one, and
so did he, after all.

"That was just fine," he said, his voice ringing through the auditorium. "So let's quit while we're ahead. Choir dismissed."

"I'm sorry I came in here," Nim said.

"Are you?"

"For intruding on your privacy, yes. I didn't realize it until you came down the aisle."

"Did you like what you heard, at least?"

"Very much. If I closed my eyes it was like the Vienna Choir Boys."

"Better," he said. "These kids know what life's about. And that's where real singing comes from."

"Cowboys and Indians," Nim said.

He grunted, caught.

"Forgive me again," Nim said.

The auditorium was empty except for the girl who collected the music and Sister Justine who seemed uncertain of whether she should go or stay.

McMahon got up. "Come back to the rectory and maybe Miss Lalor will give us a cup of tea."

In the courtyard, Nim said, "Father McMahon . . ."

He looked at her sidewise.

"I can't call you Joe in that." She traced the shape of his collar, her hand at her own neck. "I wanted to tell you—I don't know if it will mean anything, but after you left yesterday, I was thinking about Stu and the things you and I had said. I remembered there was a showing of Tchelit-chew drawings at the Burns Gallery. I went there at noon. Gustave Muller signed the visitors' book the day of the opening, a week ago Tuesday."

"So you see," McMahon said slowly, "he *had* begun a new phase of work." It did not necessarily follow, but he wanted her to believe it.

"But what you said about someone's finding him, that's where it could have happened, don't you think?"

"Yes. How many people signed the book?"

"Eighty or so. And not everybody who goes to an opening signs in. Especially when it's not new work."

"Still, I suppose we ought to tell this to the police."

"I was afraid you'd say that." She threw her hair back from her shoulders.

"What have you got against the police?"

"Prejudice."

"If you were in trouble, wouldn't you call them?"

"Yes."

And that seemed to be that until at the school gate she added: "Then maybe I'd be in more trouble."

On the rectory steps she hung back. "Are you sure it's all right, bringing me home to tea?"

McMahon laughed. "Miss Lalor is not my mother, though to be sure, she sometimes thinks so. There's nothing she likes better than to serve tea—unless it's to be asked to join the party."

"Please don't ask her." A smile fidgeted at the corners of her mouth. "I might call you Joe."

"I won't ask her," he said, and touched the bell as he opened the vestibule door. He took Nim into the study where he had been working when he saw Carlos.

"Ah, it's the young lady," Miss Lalor said, coming to the door. "I'm glad you found him, miss."

"Miss Lalor, this is Miss Lavery. She was a friend of the man who was murdered."

Miss Lalor gave Nim her most sincere look of sympathy. Her commiseration was rarely in words, only sounds and attitude. Like the priests she served, she sometimes tired of the tools, but never the materials. "Sit down, dear, and I'll bring you and Father a nice cup of tea." On her way out, she paused. "Lavery—that's a North of Ireland name, isn't it?"

"My great-grandfather came from Londonderry," Nim said.

"I've seen people from the North before with black eyes," the housekeeper said. "I've been told it's the Spanish, a long way back. Well, I'll get the tea."

When she was gone, Nim said: "My grandmother was Italian. My mother's people were Jewish."

"As long as there's a bit of Irish in there somewhere, to Miss Lalor you could be Greek, Gallic or Phoenician, and you'd still be Irish."

"Unless I were black. Am I right?"

"I'm afraid so. Except that the North are black Irish," McMahon said and grinned.

Nim studied the room with open curiosity, the crucifix, the framed blessing of the parish by Pius XII, the pictures of Popes Paul and John. "He's the one," she said of John.

"Ah, yes. As Miss Lalor would say, he's the one of them all. Mind, she's a Pius the Twelfth woman herself, but she's trying her best to catch up."

Nim, her hands behind her back, and with a childish sort of swagger continued to tour the small room. Again she stopped at the crucifix.

"It can't be all that strange," McMahon said, "Irish and Italian."

"My father was an agnostic, a physicist."

"Is he dead?"

"To me—almost from the day I was born."

"And your mother?"

"She was going to one of those rejuvenation farms the last I heard, and Dad had just been made a director in Dow Chemical."

"I see," McMahon said.

"You'd be pretty blind if you didn't." She found a straight chair, not that there was any in the room that wasn't, but she chose one without arms. She tugged at the short skirt, a hopeless gesture. "I didn't expect to be invited to tea," she said.

"I like them," McMahon said of the skirts girls were wearing now.

"For shame, Father!" Then she laughed. "There's a story, but I'll tell you another time. Something more important: it's been going through my mind all afternoon. It's Tchel-itchew again. In a way he's passé now. Forgive me if I talk to you the way I'd expect you to treat me about music. I asked Mr. Burns why the exhibit. You know, so many good artists can't get a gallery, and he said it was because a collector, a friend of his, wanted it and was willing to offer some of his Tchelitchew drawings for sale. His name is Everett Wallenstein. The name is familiar but I can't place it. I'm sure Stu never mentioned it, but he didn't mention anybody, except maybe painters he thought important to me. I'd like to go and see this man, just to talk to him. But I don't want to do it alone. I don't think I could."

"All right," McMahon said. "Make the appointment and I'll go with you. Or have you done it already?"

Nim shook her head. "I wish you'd do it."

After tea they went into the office and McMahon looked up the name in the phone book. When he dialed the number he got an answering service from whom he elicited the information that Mr. Wallenstein would not be home until after six.

"Let's just go and camp on his doorstep, surprise him," Nim said.

"You're making an adventure of it."

"I don't know what I'm making. It's all instinctual. It's not like me to crash the gate. Or wasn't. I did that this afternoon too, didn't I? And me brought up on the nicest amenities."

McMahon glanced at the parish calendar for the day. He was free between six and eight o'clock if he was willing to take his supper cold after nine. "Why not?" he said. "Meet me at six-thirty in the Whelan drugstore on the corner of Eighth Street and Sixth Avenue."

10

The house on Charles Street had been beautifully restored, outside and presumably inside, the black shutters freshly painted, the brass knocker and the mail slot polished to a high gloss. McMahon lifted the latch on the gate. A hip-high fence of wrought iron bordered a garden of tulips and iris.

"I wish I'd worn my uniform," he said, in the sport jacket again.

"I almost wish you had too," Nim said. "I feel like we ought to be peddling *The Watch Tower*."

"Not in my uniform."

The doorbell chimed deep within the house.

No one came. No sound from inside. Only the rumble of traffic on Greenwich Avenue.

"The bells," Nim said nervously, "the tintinnnabulation of the bells, bells, bells."

"The Bells of St. Mary's, that's what Monsignor Casey thought we were doing. 'There's a tune to that, Joseph.'" He mimicked the old man's accent.

"You're a snob," Nim said. "Did you see *La Plume de ma Tante?* You know, the monks ringing the bells and getting carried away. Literally, all hung up on the ropes. Wild. I was in college then. I met my father in New York and he took me to see it. That was one of our few good times together."

The door opened without their having heard the man approach. He was a tall young man, quite handsome and at the moment, sweating, as though he had been interrupted in the midst of some strenuous exercise. His hair was touseled from his having pulled on a velure sweatshirt.

"Forgive the intrusion, Mr. Wallenstein," McMahon said. "We came on the chance that you might know an artist who was a friend of ours. I'm Joseph McMahon and this is Miss Lavery."

"And who is the artist?" the man asked coldly.

"That's the trouble. We're not sure of his name."

"Then how can you be sure he's an artist?" The man looked annoyed and McMahon did not blame him. But after a second or two of indecision, he said, "You may as well come in."

It wasn't camp, or what McMahon thought of as camp, but it was pure Victorian, the small, high-ceilinged parlor into which he led them. The lamp he turned on was the real Tiffany. It occurred to McMahon that he knew more about fashion and furnishings than he had been aware of knowing.

"I don't have a telephone," Nim said, an uneasy attempt at explaining why they had come without forewarning.

"That is understandable," their reluctant host said with a sudden turn of gallantry. His eyes reinforced his intention of compliment in a frank appraisal of her, head to toe. "Excuse me a moment while I get a towel." He touched his brow where the sweat was glistening. "I have a gymnasium of sorts in the basement."

When he was gone Nim said: "I really dig this place."

"I'm trying to figure out whether I do or not," McMahon said. He went closer to one of the paintings, a pastoral scene. The signature surprised him. He covered it with his hand. "Who would you say, Nim?"

She turned on another light and studied the painting for a moment. "It's way out, but I'd say..." She hesitated. "All right, I'll say it, early Kandinsky."

"Very good," Wallenstein said from the doorway.

"Am I right?" She was delighted with herself.

"My father bought that in 1912," Wallenstein said. He wiped his face and neck in the towel. His having combed his hair, the gray streaks in it showed up. Again McMahon had misjudged age. Wallenstein was in his forties. "Now about your friend."

McMahon told him of Muller's death. "I'm a priest, by the way." He had to add that, explaining why he had been taken to the dying man.

"Are you? No one turns out to be what he seems these days. I'm sorry, but I'm at a loss to know why you've come to me: I'm afraid I have not heard of Gustave Muller."

"Neither had I," Nim said, "but I lived with him for over a year."

Wallenstein did not say anything for a few seconds, but he looked at her in a way McMahon did not like, almost as though he was fantasying himself in that position. Then he said, "And whom did you think you were living with, Miss Lavery?"

"Stuart Robinson."

Wallenstein repeated the name. "That seems familiar. Perhaps I've seen his work. Why *did* you come to me?"

"He was at the opening of the Tchelitchew exhibit at the Burns Gallery."

"Ah, now I see. But my dear girl, so were a hundred or so other people."

"I wish I had gone," Nim said. "Maybe things would have turned out differently if I'd found him."

"Not if he hadn't wanted it," McMahon said.

"Poor fool, he," Wallenstein said, again with that look at the girl which made McMahon want to hit him. An irrational reaction, he knew. Was it the having of money that made the man arrogant in such a manner? Or the fact of Nim's having frankly admitted to living with a man?

"Did you admire him as an artist, Miss Lavery?"

"Yes," Nim said unhesitatingly, which seemed strange to McMahon, knowing that she had never seen Muller's work.

"I should like to see him," Wallenstein said. "But perhaps I have. How extraordinary that an artist should change his name. His technique, his medium, his philosophy, I can understand. I paint, myself, you see, and I am as jealous of my name as I am of my mistress."

McMahon said, almost before he knew he was going to say it: "Mr. Wallenstein, would you go to the city morgue with me in the morning? It's possible you would know him under yet another name."

"Yes, of course, if it's that important to you." No hesitation, and McMahon had expected it somehow. In fact, part of his intention was to discomfit the man. "Then we won't take any more of your time now. You've been very kind, sir." He got to his feet.

"Won't you have a drink? It is that time of day."

"It's past that time for me," McMahon said. "What hour may I call you in the morning?"

"After eight. Any time after eight will be fine."

When they reached the street, Nim said: "My God, the way you got me out of there, you'd have thought it was a house of prostitution."

"That was my very feeling."

Nim grinned. "He's an odd one, isn't he? Aren't you glad we came?"

"I don't know. Maybe it's just money. I spend half my life talking about it, trying to coax it out of penny banks and working people's pockets. I didn't like the man and that's a fact."

"But why?"

"I don't know why!" he exploded.

"Because he's decadent? I rather liked that. I like the filthy rich. It's the in-betweens that turn me off."

"Then go back and have a drink with him. He'd be delighted."

"Thank you very much. You've been very kind, sir. I won't take any more of your time." Having given him back his words to Wallenstein, she turned and ran for the bus that was pulling up at the corner of Greenwich Avenue. She boarded it without looking back.

McMahon walked to Eighth Avenue and then north, thinking at every tavern he passed that he needed a drink, and aware of that craven thing in him that made him watch for those with Irish names where a priest would never be allowed to put a cent on the bar. He realized then that he was in mufti. He needed a drink, but he needed more to remember that he was a priest.

11

That the mortal remains of a man should be pulled out on a tray like a slab of beef from a freezer chilled McMahon to his very bones. He felt Brogan's hand go tight on his arm to steady him. Wallenstein had gone paper pale too. McMahon stared at the tag, then the covering: the words "winding sheet" came to him, and he thought of Lazarus rising from the dead at the bidding of Christ. Thus he got through the self-imposed ordeal. Brogan had said he could wait outside, but he chose to accompany them. He had thought at first he did it to give Wallenstein moral support, but there was also a measure of self-mortification in the act.

When he had arranged with Brogan that Wallenstein should see if he could identify the victim, McMahon had told his first lie of commission: he told of the exhibit at the Burns Gallery where Muller signed his name to the visitors' book, but he attributed the discovery to himself, not Nim, whose name had not yet come into the investigation. "Remember the art books at the pawnshop? It was just a hunch."

"Sometimes they pay off. Bring him down, Father," Brogan had said.

"I thought at first I knew him," Wallenstein said when they left the morgue.

"Who did you think he was?" Brogan asked.

"A painter I studied with some years ago—at the Art Students League. But the nose—it wasn't the same, and I remember that chap's nose. I don't remember *his* name now. I would if I heard it of course."

They went into a small cell-like office within the building. A smell McMahon associated with embalming fluid stayed with him. He was glad to see Wallenstein light a cigarette.

"It would be in the school records," Brogan suggested.

"Yes, but I assure you, he is not the same man."

"As well as the names of others in the class," the detective went on doggedly. "How many?"

"Twenty or so."

"And how many people signed in at this gallery affair last week?"

"About a hundred. Ah, I see—cross-checking the names in case I'm mistaken. That is clever."

"That's how they train us, Mr. Wallenstein," Brogan said. He didn't like him either, McMahon thought, but Brogan's next question, put with the same aloofness, surprised the priest. It also told him Brogan's slant: "Have you ever come across a man named Phelan?"

"Phelan or Fallon? I knew a Steve Fallon at one time."

"What business was he in?"

"Interior design," Wallenstein said, his voice like ice. The tenor of the detective's questioning had come across to him too. He looked at his watch, a gesture Brogan ignored.

Brogan said: "Would you have any objection to telling us where you were last Friday morning from—say dawn till noon?"

"It is none of your damned business, if I may say so, sir. Three days a week, including Fridays, I rise at eight, my housekeeper brings me breakfast at eight-thirty and by nine o'clock I am in my studio on the top floor of the house I live in. Two days a week I go to Wall Street—Wallenstein and Warren. I have not varied that routine in five years."

"I've heard of Wallenstein and Warren," Brogan said with a sheepish attempt at a smile. "I've got my routine too, and the men at the top like me to stick to it." He got up and held out his hand. "No hard feelings, Mr. Wallenstein?"

Wallenstein shook the hand. McMahon noticed that afterwards Brogan flexed his fingers.

To McMahon, Brogan said: "Thanks, Father. Keep in touch."

The priest and Wallenstein walked to the parking lot in silence. Wallenstein had picked him up at the rectory and insisted on driving him back there. Before he turned the key in the ignition, Wallenstein sat a moment playing his fingers over the steering wheel, meticulously clean fingers, such as McMahon would not have expected in an artist. In a banker, yes, however. "A curious thing about the police," Wallenstein said, "they're human like the rest of us, but they don't mind our knowing it. They would have no place in a civilized society." He glanced at McMahon. "Tell me about this Lavery girl. She has the most striking face I've seen in a long while."

McMahon was nonplused at the directness of the man. Civilization, no doubt. He was caught in a civilized trap, and one to which his own vulnerability was hinge. Certainly he was not going to comment on Nim's beauty. "She came to me thinking that Muller might have been the man she knew."

"So you said. One might wonder why she did not go to the police."

"Very civilized," McMahon said curtly.

Wallenstein smiled. "Would you mind giving me her address, Father McMahon?"

"I don't think that's my place," he said, but saying it, and remembering Nim's and his last exchange, he realized that he might be assuming something that it was truly not his place to assume. Nim might want a liaison with Wallenstein. It was himself who did not want it for her.

"Perhaps then you might arrange a meeting among the three of us? You would go to dinner with me, let us say. I should like to see her painting. That's a twist, isn't it? But I am right in supposing her to be a painter, am I not?"

"Yes."

"It is very difficult for a woman to get a decent gallery. That's gauche of me. And I've not seen her work. But her recognizing that Kandinsky on my wall—it's never been exhibited, you know."

"I didn't know," McMahon said almost sullenly. He forced himself to throw off his petulence. Then it occurred to him that he would need a fairly strong pretext for contacting Nim again himself, and he knew that he wanted to. "When?"

"I'm free tonight if it can be arranged," Wallenstein said.

"I'm not." He had to chair a meeting for the school funding committee at six, and he had not yet prepared the agenda. But how he longed to foreshorten those meetings. "At least not until after seven," he amended.

"That's fine with me. I assume you can contact Miss Lavery?"

"I'll try."

Wallenstein turned on the car motor. He gave McMahon his card. "Leave the message with whoever answers and I'll pick you up at seven-thirty."

McMahon sent Nim a telegram when he got back to the rectory. Then he put her, Wallenstein, Muller, the whole affair firmly out of his mind and concentrated on his parish duties. But in the afternoon, he managed his promised visit to Phelan.

He had been transferred to a semiprivate room. A detective McMahon had not seen before was on duty. The occupant of the other bed was a dark Puerto Rican, one leg in traction. Phelan's eyes were closed. So were the detective's. McMahon visited first with the patient in traction and his voluble family who were trying vainly to keep their voices lowered. The man had fallen down an elevator shaft. That much McMahon was able to understand. He promised to tell Father Gonzales to stop by on his next rounds.

The detective opened his eyes when he heard McMahon's voice. McMahon laid his hand on Phelan's wrist. "Dan, are you awake?"

Phelan opened his eyes and McMahon waited for the detective to leave them alone. Phelan followed the man's departure until he was out of sight. "You'd think they'd have to go to the bathroom once in a while, wouldn't you?"

"How do you feel?"

"Thoughtful. I guess that's the word. I've been lying here trying to figure out what it's all about, my marriage, my life that's been handed back to me in a glass tube."

McMahon pulled up the chair the detective had been sitting in. But he put his foot on it, the newspaper under his shoe. He wanted to be able to see the man while he talked.

"I wonder what else they could give me in a glass tube?" Phelan said with grim humor.

"A lot of your trouble's up here," McMahon said, pointing to his head. "That's where to work on it."

Phelan glanced at him and away. "Priscilla told you all about us. I keep forgetting that. I guess I want to."

"She told me the problem, yes. But she wants to find the solution to it. She loves you."

"Enough to give me up, do you think? To let me go?" This time Phelan looked at him.

"You'd rather do that than try to fix the problem?"

"It would be better for both of us. She needs somebody like . . . him. I'm thirty-one years old, Father. I got as far as two years at City College. I had a scholarship to St. Victor's Seminary in Pennsylvania. My mother wanted me to be a priest so badly she turned me off it."

"How badly did you want it?"

"Quite a lot. But I was scared—this thing, you know. I was scared of getting kicked out, I guess."

"And now you want your wife to kick you out."

"That's about it."

"What do you do for a living, Dan?"

"I'm a grip—a movie stagehand when I work. And when I don't work, I'm a stagehand at home. You know what I'd like, Father? Another chance at St. Victor's. Look, if God gave me another crack at life, why not at the seminary? It wouldn't be the first time the church annulled a marriage on those grounds."

"That wouldn't solve your problem, Dan, and now you've added a history to it with this mess."

"Look, Father, this mess has castrated me. No problem—except Priscilla."

"When you're up and around again, you may feel differently. Mind now, I'm not saying you should stay married. That's something we don't have to meet for a while. I'll make a bargain with you: promise me you'll see a doctor I've got in mind, and I'll make inquiries about St. Victor's. If there's any chance, the doctor's word would go a long way in your favor."

"Let me think about it," Phelan said.

"I'll think about it too," McMahon said.

"Priscilla doesn't need me. She's got the house and some other real estate."

"She needs you."

"How?"

"Let me ask you a question, Dan: why did you marry her?"

Phelan stared at the chart at the bottom of his bed. "Mother love."

"All right. There's lots of reasons people marry. For her it could have been vice versa."

"But for her it's not enough. She wants another kid so she'd have two of us." He pounded his fist on the bed. "For Christ's sake, Father, get me out of it!"

What God has bound together, let no man put asunder. McMahon said, "Take it easy, Dan. I'll stop by tomorrow."

12

Nim was watching for them from the window high above. When McMahon stepped from the car she called out to him and waved. The children of the street gathered around Wallenstein's black Jaguar and examined it with awe: a horse would scarcely have given them more pleasure. Wallenstein kept a tight smile going, more teeth than heart, McMahon thought. One youngster, seeing the priest go up the steps, jerked his thumb at the car. *"Agente funerario."*

He waited at the top step. The hall door was propped open. Nim came swinging down the stairs, a blur at first of yellow and red. She slowed down and became a picture. Which was not her intention. She was shy of the man who waited there. "Good evening, Father McMahon." He had come dressed as a cleric, fortified in the armor of God.

"I'm sorry I was such a fool," he said of their last meeting.

"Comédie Humaine," she murmured. "Did he recognize Stu?"

"No."

"Then what are we celebrating?"

"Experience. I'll explain that later. He hopes to be invited to view your painting—after dinner."

Nim tossed back her hair as they went out the door. "That will depend entirely on the celebration."

Some of the boys who had gathered around the big car whistled, and one, a gamin of twelve or so, skipped to the door ahead of McMahon and opened it.

Nim stuck her tongue out at him as she swept in.

Wallenstein, almost elegantly casual in dress and manner, proved himself a host of similar bent. He took them to the Trattore Gatti on Fortieth Street. Over cocktails which, he said, he drank with practiced disapproval—as an aside, he expounded on the martini as being much less a duller of the palate than sherry—he drew them out on their tastes in food. Nim liked everything except liver.

"Especially paté." Wallenstein said. "It's like coating your tongue with velvet." They agreed to his ordering the dinner for all of them.

With the second martini they had oysters, with the pasta, oil and garlic sauce only, the poor man's spaghetti, McMahon thought, but with such a difference here—a Soave wine. When the *osso bucco* came, Wallenstein unbuttoned the cuffs of his British suit and turned them up while he disjointed and served the knuckles. The maître d' came to watch a craftsman at work. The waiter showed the claret bottle, but McMahon missed the label, leaning over to hear Nim whisper, "Dago red."

What had they talked about? McMahon wondered afterwards. He became a little drunk, as much with the food and the talk as the drinks, and he thought about the pleasure it would give him to recite the menu in every detail to the monsignor. He talked of Lili Boulenger and the trenchant music she had composed, so young, so ill. Wallenstein was delighted with his use of the word, trenchant, to describe music. "I knew this dinner would pay off," he said, but with such deliberate overexposure of self-interest that it seemed ingratiating. And Nim talked about her tutelage as a painter under Stuart Robinson. Trenchant, she felt, was a good word for his approach to art also. Then, in a kind of haze, McMahon heard her tell of her father's test as to whether she was an artist. He had taken her to see a Professor Broglio with whom he had studied as a boy.

"He wanted to know by what right I thought I had sufficient talent."

"Sufficient talent for what?" Wallenstein asked.

"To measure in dollars and cents," Nim said. "That's

how to calculate a woman's work. A man's can be a long-term investment." She was lucid if not faultless in her syllogism.

Wallenstein clicked his tongue at the cynicism. "And what did the professor say?"

"He said, 'Lavery, how do you know you cannot play the violin?' 'I just know it,' my father said. 'Any fool would know it the moment I picked one up.' 'Any fool but you,' Professor Broglio said. 'If you had it in you to play the violin, you would know it. It would only be a matter of learning how.'"

"Bully for him," Wallenstein said. "Father McMahon has told you that I would like to see your painting?" Suave as Soave, McMahon thought.

He pondered these fragments of their dinner talk as they drove downtown again. Both the beguilement and the booze were wearing off. The man was an enigma, and the whole experience of having sprung an evening such as this from a five-minute intrusion into his parlor seemed a kind of madness. Will you come into my parlor, said the spider. . . . He glanced at Nim who sat between them on the wide seat. She was holding herself, prim as a spinster, as Miss Lalor might, touching neither of them with arm, elbow or thigh.

"Contrast, the only true measure of enjoyment," Wallenstein said, turning into Fifth Street.

"I don't think my neighbors would appreciate the esthetic," Nim said. "But it suits me fine."

"Aren't you afraid, living here?"

"Sometimes. But not of my neighbors."

"Of what?"

She shrugged. "I guess of the people who come here to get away from respectability."

"Like me, for example."

"I hadn't thought of you that way."

"You are right. I am not that respectable," Wallenstein said, all quiet as though McMahon was not in the car at all.

Nim, with the forthrightness McMahon admired in her,

said: "Do you really want to see my painting, Mr. Wallenstein?"

He took his eyes from the street for a moment and turned toward her. "Only if you want me to."

So, McMahon decided, whether he liked it or not, he had to give Wallenstein the benefit of the doubt.

Nim turned on all the lights and took her canvases from the rack, setting out three or four of them at a time, propping them against the beams, a chair she had brought from the kitchen, and the rattan rocker. McMahon and Wallenstein sat on the edge of the bed.

Wallenstein said nothing at first, but got up now and then to see a particular picture from another angle. He moved the lamps around to his own satisfaction. "Set that one aside," he said now and then so that when she had shown some thirty canvases in all and said herself that it was enough, he had picked out ten that he wanted to look at again.

McMahon found himself looking inward more than at the pictures. He simply could not relate. It distressed him, for he had wanted very much to see and like Nim's work. Why, God knew, but suddenly he was remembering the picture of the Sacred Heart that hung in the Morales house, and he wondered what they had done with the effigy of Muller.

"Have you shown at all, Miss Lavery?" Wallenstein could not have been more formal, McMahon thought, forcing himself back to the present.

"In a couple of group shows on Tenth Street," Nim said. "I've sold three paintings."

"From this period?" He indicated the pictures he had wanted set aside.

"Yes, as a matter of fact."

"Fortunate buyers. You ought to have a gallery, young lady."

Nim sat down in the rocker, smiling a little, a remote look in her eyes. It was not so much remoteness, McMahon decided then, but more, as she glanced toward her work, a private involvement. Finally she said, "I was thinking. I'm not that young—as your young lady, and I was glad I'm not."

A strange thing happened: At a little sound from Wallenstein, McMahon looked at him. The man's eyes were watery. Wallenstein got up from the bed and went to Nim, and taking her hand, he lifted it briefly to his lips.

"I weep for myself, you know that, don't you?" He blew his nose. "Well. I am not an entrepreneur, but I do have friends. Thank you very much." He turned abruptly to McMahon. "Shall I drop you at the rectory, Father?"

"Please stay, Father McMahon," Nim said, "just for a little while."

McMahon said, "I'll walk home, thank you. I often walk the streets at night."

"That's where the message is," Wallenstein said, and put out his hand.

McMahon felt the almost hurtful clasp of a hand you would have thought would go limp in yours. He remembered Brogan flexing his fingers.

At the door Wallenstein paused. "May I ask, Miss Lavery, what does your father think of your painting now?"

"My father?" Nim said. "I've never shown it to him."

"Why?"

Nim shrugged and thought about it. "I guess it's my own kind of revenge."

"I like you," he said. "I wish we could be friends."

McMahon was not looking at them, only listening, but he could imagine Wallenstein's eyes on him, the guardian of honor.

When she closed the door after he had gone down the first two flights, Nim went to the window and looked down. He would have looked up, for presently she waved.

McMahon stared at the one painting facing him, blues and black and many greens: a fish? a raft afloat in the changing sea? a coffin?

Nim came and stood beside him. "What are you thinking?" She nodded at the picture.

"Just wondering..." He did not want to admit his literalness.

But she knew it anyway. "What do you want it to be?"

"Is that the criterion?"

"It's as good as any," she said. "I'm that way about music, poetry. Stu used to say that most artists are conservative about every art except their own. Please take off the collar. I want to call you Joe." She put away the canvases. "I suppose you've guessed by now, I mixed them up, but every painting he selected came out of the time Stu and I were together."

McMahon put his collar and the stud in his pocket. "What do you think that means?"

"One of two things," Nim said. "Either he knew Stu and isn't admitting it—or he knows painting and I'm good."

"I prefer that interpretation."

Nim smiled. "I'd suggest a drink, but gin would be sinful after a meal like that. Wasn't it the most?"

"It was a lot," McMahon said, "and for once I didn't hate myself, piling it in."

"Why do you hate yourself for that? Penance?"

"Pride. The handout. You know, nothing but the best for the priest, free. I'm afraid pride is my hangup on the road to—wherever I'm trying to go."

"Nothing but the best for the artist," Nim said with a defiant thrust of her chin, "and he damned well deserves it. Mr. Wallenstein got his money's worth out of both of us tonight, Joe. Maybe he cries easier than I think he does, but tears aren't anything money can turn on." She laughed. "It can't turn them off either."

"That sounds Talmudic," McMahon said.

"My Jewish grandparents."

McMahon did not say anything.

"You want to get out of here, don't you?" she said after a moment. "Let's walk. Let's turn another table: I'll walk *you* home."

"That's not a very good idea at this hour," he said.

"For the love of God, don't go fatherly on me. Let's just walk." She took up her red stole from the bed.

When they reached the street Nim paused on the stoop and breathed deeply. "I'm getting expert at holding my breath. But I don't mind the smell so much, not really. And my place is nice, don't you think?"

"I think it's beautiful."

"Then why wouldn't you tell me until I asked you?"

McMahon shrugged. "I suppose because I never think such things are expected of me."

"And don't you ever do things that aren't expected of you?"

"I try not to," he said truculently.

"Forgive me. I'm a curious sort of person. I ask too many questions."

They crossed the street. Nim paused at the gates of the Orthodox Church. "Are you willing? I'd love to show you. I sometimes come here alone at night."

"Isn't it locked?"

"I know where the key is. Stu was custodian, remember? And after he went away, I asked for the job. The old priest was shocked, but I think he'd have given it to me if it weren't for his wife."

"All right," McMahon said. Waiting at the top of the steps while she groped the frame of the side door for the cutout where the key was concealed, he subconsciously reverted to the self he was at the moment of entry into the holiest of places.

Inside, the door closed behind them, they stood in silence in the presence of—what? Scented ghosts of ancient saints, their icons palely glittering in the light of glass-bound candles.

McMahon said the words aloud: "I will go unto the altar of God, to God who gives joy to my youth."

"That's lovely," Nim said softly. "What is it?"

"It's the opening of the old Mass. It's been changed now. It's not the same."

"Why did they change it?"

"I don't know. Nothing's the same—for me." He realized as he said it that it was true: he was as reactionary about the liturgy as the monsignor. And what was liturgy but form, and therefore was it the forms only that bound him in his faith? "I believe..." he said aloud but again speaking to himself. He held out his hands and turned them slowly in the flickering light; he shaped a crescent, with the consecrated fingers, the miracle-making hands in which the bread became the body of Christ. He gathered them into fists. "I do believe."

"In God, in joy, in youth," Nim said. "What else is there?"

"Love."

"That's what it's all about, isn't it?"

"I hope that is so," he said. He would have liked to pray, but for that he needed a church of his own, and that he knew to be the answer to the question he had asked himself about the forms. He had expected, he admitted now, the flesh to be his greatest temptation, but it was not. How long he stood there, his fists tight against himself, he did not know. "I need to go home," he said. "Wherever that is."

"I understand. And you want to go alone."

"Yes."

"Then go," she said quietly. "I'll stay here for a while. I only wish I could take you where I think it is."

"God bless you, Nim. You are a fine person."

"I am blessed and I am damned," she said. "Good-bye, Joe."

"Good night. That's all. Just good night." He groped his way along the back wall until he found the door for himself.

The monsignor's bedroom door was open at the top of the stairs, his light on. Everyone else had gone to bed. McMahon tapped at the door. It was expected of him, whether he had been to a wake or a concert, if the light was on. When he went in the old man was propped up in bed, his breviary in hand, his glasses halfway down his nose.

McMahon sat on the bedside chair and told him about the dinner which, in the perspective of what happened afterward, had lost its flavor. He was primed by his audience, however, and he took an almost wicked pleasure in coaxing the old man into the savoring of it.

"Did they open the oysters at the table? I've seen that done, you know." Then later, marking his place in the book with the faded red ribbon and setting it aside, the old man said, "Joseph . . ." and hesitated as though not sure of how to get into a delicate subject.

McMahon steeled himself. He had explained the dinner party as growing out of Nim's feeling that Wallenstein might have known Muller. Now he expected to be questioned on Nim and his involvement in the whole affair. On the long walk home he had made up his mind and he was prepared now to say that he did not intend to see her again.

But the monsignor said, "Wallenstein . . . it's an old name in New York finance. Is he part of the family?"

"I don't know," McMahon lied. He knew then what was coming, and he tried to stem the rise of his own anger.

"A dinner like that, Joseph?"

"There is money," he said.

"I would think so—and a patron of the arts. Did you talk about music?"

"Yes, Monsignor."

"Some of our greatest benefactors are Jewish, you know. It's their way of making up."

"For what?"

The old man looked at him over his glasses. "Joseph," he said in a tone that warned of his temper's rising.

But McMahon said, "I thought it was we who were trying to make up to them these days."

"That was not my meaning and you know it, Joseph. If you had to deal night and day with the support of a parish as I do—yes, I'll say it to you—if you lived up to the talents God gave you for directing a parish instead of diddling on that piano in there, if you left the highfalutin music to Carnegie Hall and taught the girls the songs of their own people that'd keep them singing at home and off the streets, then you'd be doing a priest's work."

"Yes, Monsignor," McMahon said tightly.

"How much did you get pledged at the meeting for the renovation of the school?"

"Not very much. I'll have the report on your desk in the morning."

"You've the time to write me reports, but not to tell me what happened," the old man said, revealing the true source of his wrath, McMahon's remoteness.

"There's a question on whether the school should be renovated, Monsignor."

"Would they have it fall in on the children's heads?"

"They recommended the referral of the matter to the archdiocese with the reminder that a new public school is about to be built within two blocks of the parish."

"They'd close the school?" the old man said in slow disbelief. Then: "Over my dead body! I've put twenty years of my life into this parish, and by the glory of God, if I've seen it integrated, I won't see it disintegrated." His face was an apoplectic red. "For shame, Father McMahon. Will you sign the report?"

"It's not my place, Monsignor."

"I'm to sign my own death warrant, am I? Isn't that what it amounts to?"

McMahon, his temper overcome by sympathy, said: "You'd be humiliated, Monsignor, having to go to the cardinal for three quarters of the money. There's no hope of raising more than a quarter of it in the parish."

"There's always a way. It's a matter of asking the right people when you know them."

McMahon could say nothing except, "Good night, Monsignor."

"Good night, good night . . ." But when McMahon reached the door, he said after him, "You don't want to beg from a Jew. Is that it, Joseph?"

"Maybe that's it," he said to get out. "Or maybe it's just

that I don't want to beg any more." He closed the door after him.

In the hallway he saw Miss Lalor bumping down from her end of the house in her tent of a bathrobe, her hair as wild as a bunch of heather.

"It's all over," he said, "Good night, Miss Lalor."

But she had to say her piece too. "The two of you, shouting at the top of your voices. Isn't there enough of that on the streets, Father?"

"Mind your own business," McMahon said. "You are not my mother."

In his room he took his collar from his pocket and looked at it and then put it away for another wearing.

13

Phelan's eyes were open when McMahon visited him the next day. "Father, I'll see that doctor of yours, if you'll get rid of this bedside companion for me." He jerked his thumb at the detective who lumbered to his feet as the priest came in.

"Listen, Mac. If you think this is my idea of paradise, you're out of your ever-loving mind. You won't talk and they won't shut up." He threw a mean glance at the family reunion around the other patient.

"Have a smoke," McMahon said.

"I was off them for two weeks when I got this detail. Now I'm hooked again."

While the detective was on his way to the door, Phelan, baiting him, said after him: "That's right, man. You're really hooked." To McMahon he added, the man now out of hearing, "He's got six kids and his father-in-law lives with them."

"Which is probably why he doesn't have eight kids," McMahon said.

Phelan grinned.

"You're feeling better."

Phelan said: "Did you get in touch with St. Victor's?"

"Not yet. You told me you wanted to think about it. I did call a friend in the chancery council. There are other places besides St. Victor's, if you're serious, Dan."

"If I wasn't, I wouldn't be seeing this doctor you talk about. Is he a Catholic?"

"Yes."

"There aren't many of them, are there—Catholic head-shrinkers?"

"They don't shrink heads. They open you up so that you can look for yourself."

"That's even worse."

"What have you been doing these last few days lying here?"

"Trying to look. That's the truth," Phelan said after a moment.

"All he'll do is throw a little light your way. It's not like going to confession, Dan. It's not that at all. It may turn out he'll show you a lot of the things you're feeling guilty about are not a matter for confession at all."

Phelan looked up at him sharply. "Man, you're the new church, aren't you, Father?"

McMahon smiled. "Half and half." He did not want to think about himself. He had spent too much of the night doing that, half on his knees and half on his back, fighting fantasies he could not elude. Even the scriptures fed them: Nim-Naomi—even that. And the whole Orthodox church in the darkness when he had supposed his temptation to be of the spirit and not the flesh, turning to it as a counter-temptation—fighting fire with fire—he had remembered how he came to the church in the first place, Rosenberg's saying that Muller and the girl had probably made love there: a joke on the pawnbroker's part, but the joker in McMahon's house of cards which he had built, thinking it the house of God. He turned away from the bed and the thoughtful man lying in it and saw the family who waited the moment he would come to them. A chorus of responses to the merest of his attentions. "Look, Father!" A child wheeled the pulley supporting his father's leg, sending it slowly up a few inches and then down again, proving to all the man's improvement.

"Congratulations," McMahon said. "I'll come over in a minute."

"Father," Phelan said, "tell the police I have nothing to

give them. I did not kill him. I'd have killed my wife first. Say that to them and they'll understand it. I've got it all figured out, lying here—the way they think."

"Dan, I'll get Doctor Connelly here as soon as I can. That will impress them, that and another suspect if we can find one."

"Do you think I should go to confession?"

"Do you think so yourself?" McMahon did not want to confess him: he wanted to hear no more now about the sexual problems of man or woman.

"Maybe I'd better wait and see what this doctor has to say."

"Good man," McMahon said, and brushed Phelan's cheek with his knuckles. "Meanwhile, I'll go round and speak to Traynor."

He spent a few minutes with the Puerto Rican family, basking, refreshing himself in the warmth of their welcome.

As he was about to leave the room, Phelan said: "You won't forget St. Victor's?"

"No."

"I want it a lot, Father."

"I want it for you too." Then he added: "If it's what you want." But he realized as he said it that he wanted it for himself: he was trying to provide the church with a substitute priest.

He used the hospital phone to call the psychiatrist, aware of the dime it saved him. Dr. Connelly, hearing as much of Phelans' history as the priest could give him, agreed to stop at St. Jude's sometime that afternoon. McMahon did not like himself for thinking it, but he suspected it was the police aspect of the case that made it more attractive to a man as busy as Connelly. But then McMahon did not like himself for anything just now.

He walked from the hospital to precinct headquarters. Brogan and Traynor were in a meeting, but when the sergeant phoned up that Father McMahon was at the desk, he was told to send him up.

"We've got a line on him, Father," Brogan said as soon as he walked into the office. "No matter what kind of a copout he was trying to pull, you can't fool the FBI."

McMahon felt a sinking sense of disappointment, disillusionment, and he thought at once of Nim.

Traynor, with his quick, appraising eye, saw the change of expression on the priest's face. "What Brogan is saying, Father—we've been able to trace the victim through his fingerprints, an operation coordinated by the Federal Bureau of Investigation."

"Oh," McMahon said, his relief in his voice.

Traynor was not a man to be gratuitously kind. "It's got through to you, hasn't it, Father?—my enemy the cop, the FBI, the Establishment. That's what we are now, the Establishment. Brogan, how does it feel to be part of the Establishment on eight thousand bucks a year?"

"I don't get it," Brogan said.

"I don't either," Traynor said, "a priest on the side of anarchy."

From their first meeting, McMahon thought, he and Traynor had rubbed one another the wrong way: there was nothing reasonable in their reaction to one another; it was almost chemical, and what the lieutenant had just said came out of that polarization. He said now, "Lieutenant, we've got to live by communication. I believe that, and I don't think that's anarchy. For my part, I'm trying to communicate on both levels." Then, hypocrite or pragmatist, he added: "Monsignor Casey sends you his warmest, by the way."

"Thank you. Fill him in, Brogan. I'll get in touch with Wisconsin. Maybe we'll have a vacancy in the morgue if nothing else before the day's over."

At another desk in the office Brogan showed McMahon the teletype transcript of the information turned up through the fingerprint search. It had come through Selective Service records. The man they knew as Muller had been born in Madison, Wisconsin, August 13, 1925, Thomas Stuart

Chase. He had served as a lieutenant during the occupation of Germany following World War II. Honorably discharged, he had returned to Europe on the G.I. Bill to study painting. His next of kin was listed as an aunt, Muriel Chase of Madison.

"Where do you go from here?" McMahon asked.

"Aunt Muriel, if she's still alive," Brogan said. "But with his real name to work on, we have several directions— Social Security records for one, if he ever worked for a living."

McMahon refused himself the indulgence of any more arguments with the police. "What about Phelan?"

Brogan shrugged. "He still won't talk. Ask the boss."

A few minutes later McMahon did go over the Phelan situation with Traynor. Not his interest in the priesthood, but the fact that he would be under the care of Dr. Gerald Connelly. A premature statement, but he was himself satisfied in the likelihood of its happening.

"You don't think he'll make another attempt at suicide?"

"I do not."

Traynor was more flexible than he had anticipated. "I'll go along with your thinking, Father." To Brogan he said, "Cancel the detail. But when he gets out of the hospital, put a tail on him. Maybe his feet will talk if his tongue won't."

"Thank you, lieutenant," McMahon said.

"Thank *you,* Father."

When McMahon got back to the rectory after classes that afternoon he found a note tacked to the door of his room to call Detective Brogan. Whenever Miss Lalor was miffed with him, she pinned his messages to the door. Otherwise, she delivered them in person, deciphering them from amongst her shopping notes. He called Brogan.

"There's an Aunt Muriel all right," Brogan said. "She's on her way East now. I told her you wanted to arrange a funeral service and she said to go ahead. She'll take the ashes back to Wisconsin with her."

McMahon was stunned. The so-called memorial at the Morales house had been sufficient to the wishes of Muller's neighbors, and certainly to his own involvement. But Brogan had not known that. "I'll call Ferguson and Kelly," he said mechanically.

"Let me know when. Call me right back on it, Father. The boss wants a notice in the papers. It might turn up some interesting people."

And there he was, McMahon thought, being used again by the police. But that's what a priest was for, to be used by those who needed him. Even the police. Humility, Joseph. Your name saint was a humble man. Remember that . . . and he was used if ever a man was. He thought about that: he could not stem the flow of cynicism now. It was as though he had opened the floodgates. He tried to remember what it was exactly that Martin Luther had said at the end of his life about being powerless to close them; and even in the wake of this thought came further skepticism: Luther had not wanted to close them, but sentimental Catholic historians had perpetuated the legend.

He made the funeral arrangement for four o'clock the following day, Friday. And its being the first Friday of the month, he would have it announced at the morning Masses so the word would reach the tenement house without his having to go there. He called Brogan back.

McMahon sat on at the office desk, his head in his hands. Phelan was not the only one who needed help. Father Purdy looked in and asked if there was anything he could do. "Pray for me," McMahon said, and God must know it was an act of humility to ask the prayers of Father Purdy.

He composed a telegram to Nim and phoned it in: "Funeral Muller born Thomas Stuart Chase Friday 4 P.M. Ferguson and Kelly Parlor."

Where, telegraphing her about meeting Wallenstein, he had worried about the item on the parish phone bill, it scarcely entered his mind now.

After choral practice he went again to see Abel Rosenberg.

"I suppose I knew he was over there," Rosenberg said. "I have made some notes. Words on paper, that is all. A man's conversation, it is not the way it looks in books." He took a notebook from the middle drawer of the desk and opened it. "For example, I have said here: When you think of concentration camps, what do you see? He asked me that. And I said—and it was very hard for me—I said, I see my sister Ida and the children, and I do not look. So, he said, put yourself there and look. And he described to me the filth, the stench, the wire, the degradation. Oh, yes. He was there. And he made me transport myself there. All right, I said, I am there, I am there." Rosenberg's whole frail body quivered with the recollection of what another man had made him conjure. He did not look at the priest, he stared ahead, conjuring against the background of the desk with all its cubicles. "I remember saying, each one of these"—he put his finger to one after another of the cubicles—"is a bunk and there are so many of us our bodies touch, always touch and stick and stink. And he said, what are you doing? You are there, but what are you doing inside you? I am surviving. I am thinking of a red rose I once gave my mother on her birthday. Describe it, he said. And I described it, the silken petals, the color of heart's blood, the leaves, the fragrance, the thorns . . . And he said, That is art and where it comes from. And so we had a cognac and I was an artist. Will you have a cognac, Father?"

McMahon was a moment realizing that the last words were addressed to him. "No, thank you, Mr. Rosenberg."

"What else?" He looked again at the notebook. "The picture Hitler wanted. He told me about a painter he knew who had won a prize in Austria and how one of the German collectors so admired it he ordered the gallery to send it to the Fuehrer for his private collection. The artist himself went into the gallery that night and slashed it into a hundred shreds. 'Why did he do that, do you think?' Gust asked me. 'It is obvious,' I said. 'He did not want Hitler to have it.' 'Or was it this, Rosenberg? If the picture was good enough for Hitler, it was no longer good enough for him? That is why I would have destroyed it.' Something like that, he said."

McMahon said: "Do you think that's what he did? Destroy his own painting?"

"The same thought has come into my head, Father. And I think it is possible that he did that."

"This changing of identity, dropping out and starting over."

"A pursuit of absolute beauty," Rosenberg said.

"That's enough to destroy a man in itself," McMahon said, and thought again of Muller's words, I took the knife away from him. Had he wanted to die? Had his killer done him a kindness in those terms? Was that the meaning of his silence, his refusal to name the man? "No," he said aloud, getting up with Rosenberg because someone had come into the shop. "I don't believe he wanted to die."

"It was the opposite, Father. He was destroying himself because he wanted to live."

"I found the girl, by the way—Nana Marie. You will like her. I think she'll come to the funeral."

"Then I will come also, and you will play Bach and Mahler after all."

That night, after confessions were over and the church emptied of people, he took the score for "Song of Earth" which he had borrowed from the library, and his own copy of Bach's "Jesu, Joy of Man's Desiring" to the choir loft and practiced them on the organ. When he came downstairs he found the monsignor sitting in the back pew. The old man got up, steadying himself on the bench.

"That was beautiful, Joseph. I am sorry for what I said last night about your diddling on the piano."

McMahon said, "Give me your blessing, Monsignor."

He knelt and the old man touched his forehead, crossing it with his thumb and said the words in the Latin beloved to both of them. McMahon kissed his hand.

14

Only a few people came to the funeral, Mrs. Morales with Carlos, the boy in his first communion suit, Mrs. Phelan came with two other women of the building. McMahon realized he had not seen her during his recent visits to the hospital. He said the obvious by way of greeting, "Dan is much better."

"You saved him, Father," she said, a little curl of irony at the corners of her mouth.

Rosenberg came, but Nim had not when it was time to begin the service. The newspapers were represented. A photographer snapped a picture of Traynor and Brogan when they entered the chapel with a woman McMahon assumed to be Muller-Chase's aunt. She was large—not stout, but big-boned—fairly on in her sixties and well-dressed in a way that fashion would not interfere with. Traynor introduced her to the priest whom she acknowledged as "Reverend." Neither cordial nor aloof, she was, McMahon felt, as cautious with her commitments to people as her nephew had been casual with his. Out of the numerous available chairs—the casket was discreetly out of sight behind curtains in the apse of the room—she chose to sit next to Rosenberg, and McMahon mused on what other circumstance under the sun would have brought two people of such disparate backgrounds together. Rosenberg got to his feet at her approach and then sat down again when she did.

McMahon read from the Psalms and then from the Book of Ruth, the passage including the words, "And thy people shall be my people." He thought of Nim, but that was not why he had selected it: it led him into what he knew of this man who was loved by the strangers whom he chose time and again as his people. He spoke briefly and then said that at the request of a friend he was going to play some music. Before he had reached the organ at the back of the chapel Brogan and Traynor left. As he started to play, Nim came in and sat down.

Miss Chase turned in her chair to look at the girl. McMahon was reminded of all the matron ladies who turned purposefully in church to show their disapproval of latecomers, and there flashed through his mind the picture of this woman in some Fundamentalist congregation where, for a lifetime, she would have sat in the same pew every Sunday and after every service complimented the minister at the door on the excellence of his sermon.

Mrs. Phelan, Mrs. Morales and the other women of the building fled the chapel as soon as McMahon got up from the organ—like Catholics at the *Ita, Missa est,* Go, the Mass is finished. And he remembered the impish glee with which, among all altar boys, he too had sung out the Thanks be to God. In the presence of the dead he almost always thought of childhood. There came back to his mind then that last picture of Muller, turning his head in on his wounded self.

He moved quickly to Nim and took her to meet Miss Chase who was introducing herself to Rosenberg as they went up.

"Only a friend," Rosenberg said of himself.

"Miss Chase," McMahon said, "may I present Miss Lavery, another friend of your nephew's?"

She appraised the girl with one swift glance, wise eyes; not unkind, just satisfying herself. She murmured the amenity and turned to McMahon. "It was a lovely service, Reverend McMahon, but I had thought my nephew to be an atheist."

"He may have been, but I don't know any prayers in that language."

Nim and Rosenberg were amused, but Miss Chase followed in her own train of thought. "The Chases have been Congregationalists for generations. But Tom made his own choices from the cradle—if not to the grave." Her expression showed the turning off of futile memories. "There were very few I approved of and I see no reason to be hypocritical about it now."

"How long has it been since you saw him?" McMahon asked.

"Over twenty years. He came home briefly after the war. But he wanted to live in Paris. So, I let him go. Not that I could have stopped him. But it was painful letting go—the last of the Chase name." She stood a moment, making up her mind whether to go on. Another quick glance at Nim seemed to decide her. "I was his guardian and I consented to give him the money left in my trust. We had argued it at some length. I borrowed on the securities rather than sell them, and finally I was able to put the check for the full inheritance in his hands. Whereupon he tore it up and put it back in mine. And left with an army knapsack on his back, although he had been an officer. But I was thinking, Reverend McMahon, while you spoke: does he have an heir? Will one now show up, or several perhaps? Is there someone who will come some day to see me and call me Aunt Chase—as he did—never Aunt Muriel?"

"I don't know," McMahon said.

She looked at Nim for whom the question had been intended in the first place.

"I know of none, Miss Chase," Nim said, "but then I only knew him for a year or so."

"Did you really know him, child?"

"I knew . . . someone," Nim said.

"We all knew someone," Rosenberg said, "but who did we know?"

"A kind man in any case," McMahon said.

"You have a peculiar notion of kindness, Reverend McMahon, if I may say so." And reaching out the gloved hand, she put one finger under Nim's chin and lifted it. "Look at this girl's face and tell me if it was a kind man she knew."

"He was," Nim said although her eyes filled with tears. "It was just that he went away—and he wasn't coming back."

"I said that twenty years ago, but I didn't believe it either. Now it is so. I'll give you my address if you would like to write to me, Miss Lavery..."

Nim shook her head.

"I think I understand," the older woman said. "Now I suppose I must speak to these newspaper people. I said I would after the service." She drew a deep breath. "Tom was a painter—but what did he paint?"

"He *was* a painter," Nim said. "You must believe that, Miss Chase."

"I do believe it. One of his few communications in all these years was a note saying he thought I would approve his present situation: he was teaching in the art department at Columbia University.... Which is why I mistook you, Mr. Rosenberg..."

"Just a friend," Rosenberg said again.

"I have decided to offer a reward," she said, "after discussing it with the police. I would like very much to have something painted by Thomas Stuart Chase. I do not like publicity. But in this case, I like the lack of it even less." She shook hands with Nim and Rosenberg, and then taking off her glove, she gave her hand to McMahon. But first she slipped a folded bill out from the other glove and put it in his hand. "You will have many charities. I have few."

McMahon murmured his thanks and put the money in his coat pocket without looking at it. His mother had always tucked something into that pocket when they parted. He tried to think of that and not of the fives and tens pressed upon him by strangers who were so moved by his participation in an intimate moment of their lives. It always nicely separated participation from sharing.

McMahon went to the chapel door with her and then returned to where Rosenberg was telling Nim of the art books left in his keeping. McMahon realized they had had to introduce themselves.

"Rightly they belong to Miss Chase," Nim said.

"Rightly? What is rightly? Young lady, he would not have approved that kind of shilly-shally. I wish you to have them."

"Thank you," Nim said. "I want them very much."

McMahon both dreaded and looked forward to this moment, just the meeting of eyes with Nim, but it passed with a kind of glancing off. "So now we know something we didn't know before, Columbia University."

"Crazily, I know someone there," Nim said. "Or did. Remember my telling Mr. Wallenstein about my father taking me to see Professor Broglio? That was at Columbia. And if that old man isn't dead, he might still be there."

"I would suppose, Miss Nim," Rosenberg said, "you think people to be a lot older than they are. I know I did at your age. May I offer you both a cognac? My brother-in-law is in the shop, but it will be time to close soon. Then you can take some of the books home with you."

McMahon consulted his datebook on the rest of the day's schedule. He had been going to see Phelan, but he had nothing more to tell him and he was now in Dr. Connelly's care. McMahon hoped that it was so. In the parish hall it was bingo night, and that could go on very nicely without his blessing. "I think it's exactly what we need," he said.

There was something in walking into the back of that shop with its old-fashioned desk, the chairs with their seats hollowed by a thousand sittings, the brass-knobbed cupboards, the green lamps, the orchestra of musical instruments temporarily put by, something that sent him back in history, that in truth released him from the tensions of his own place and time.

When Rosenberg had brought the cognac bottle and the glasses and took his place in the swivel chair, his white hair fairly shone beneath the glow of the lamp. McMahon said to Nim: "Our friend thought of Rembrandt, sitting here where we are. What was it he said, Mr. Rosenberg?"

"That Rembrandt would have painted me one of his famous Jews."

"I'm part Jewish," Nim said.

Rosenberg looked at her gravely. "So who would he have painted you? What was the name of the woman at the half door?"

Nim shook her head. "No half doors for me."

She would not look at McMahon but the color rose to her face.

Rosenberg said, "So we drink again to our strange and lovable friend." He sipped and smacked his lips. "Our friend who got faces all mixed up in the roots of things. I have made another note or two. Rooting among the roots. He would like that, to play with words. He did not like nature, and I would make a bet with you: the aunt is an outdoors woman. A grower of roses maybe."

"The faces mixed up in the roots of things," Nim said. "That's Tchelitchew again."

"Tchelitchew," Rosenberg repeated. "That's the name. You will laugh at me like he did. I have written down Charlie Chan. Rembrandt I know, but Tchelitchew is a foreigner—to Abel Rosenberg. He went to see this Tchelitchew and he said it was a terrible mistake. He said a man should not try to run from the devil. He should open his arms."

McMahon and Nim looked at each other. "So there it is," she said, "but what is it?"

"That's police work, Nim. They'll go over that list with a fine-tooth comb."

Nim nodded. "I don't know why, but I don't feel revengeful. I just want to know about him, Stu . . . Mr. Rosenberg is right on how he felt about nature. It troubled him. It hurt too much. Something." She put her glass down carefully and folded her hands beneath her chin. She almost always sat in that hunched position. "I'm going to try to say something the way he said it to me once. You see, when I knew him it was this whole thing about the young people in the East Village he was trying to dig, the flower children, the nonviolent, the dropout. He started this way: I am an artist because I am a violent man. Most artists are. But the violence is inside them. They go among their brothers, crying 'Peace! Peace!' because they don't know peace themselves. They keep digging at their own souls. They draw the world's infections into themselves, and in the furnace of their genius they try to burn it out, to get at the essence of man."

Rosenberg said, "You got him down perfect. It is me in the concentration camp all over again."

Nim said, "There's one more line, the one about nature: Walden Pond! I would rather look in the toilet bowl."

"Oh, my, my, my," Rosenberg said and bowed his head.

Finally McMahon said: "If we could reach this Professor Broglio, Nim, would you want to talk to him—just to find out?"

"If he'd remember me," Nim said.

"Any man would remember you, Miss Nim," Rosenberg said. "Just keep this in mind, young lady: our friend remembered you or we would not be sitting here together now."

Nim smiled at him flashingly.

"May I use the phone?" McMahon said.

"Please." While McMahon drew the phone to him, Rosenberg said: "Wasn't it beautiful, the music Father played?"

"Very."

McMahon hesitated, his hand on the phone. "Something strange went through my mind while I was playing—I think Brogan and Traynor's walking out started it—but I thought: I should have been a painter, not a musician."

"A composer," Rosenberg suggested.

"No, a painter. And I wondered if it was possible for an

artist to choose the wrong medium." Not until he had dialed the operator did it occur to him that in the moment of saying that of himself he had quite forgotten his priesthood. It upset him and he avoided Nim's eyes though he felt them. He asked Information for the university number, and then said to Nim: "Tell Mr. Rosenberg what the professor said to your father."

A few minutes later McMahon had the information that Professor Broglio's schedule included a Saturday class from ten until noon.

"So," Rosenberg said, "you can go and see him again."

Nim said, "I told that story to Stu once. Professor Broglio, he said, and I said, do you know him? Only the name, Nim. Only the name. Now I wonder. He had to know him."

"Tomorrow morning. Enough till then," McMahon said.

"Always to him life was a hall of mirrors, bump, bump, bump," Rosenberg said. "A little more cognac before we close up shop. How Gust loved his cognac."

"And gin," Nim said, "and Scotch, I suppose, and Irish, and all the wines of Paris."

"It is not right for you to be bitter," the pawnbroker said. "Bitterness is judgment."

"Self-pity," Nim said. "Is that judgment? I suppose it is."

"So your father consented to your studying painting," Rosenberg gently turned the subject.

"Not bloody likely. I consented and I've paid my own way since. And I'm glad. For all the bump, bump, bumps, I like it this way."

"That is much better," Rosenberg said.

Nim looked at McMahon. "But I was thinking—what you said about the possibility of choosing the wrong art? For years and years I've wanted to be able to play the piano."

"So you will teach one another," Rosenberg said, a born fixer.

McMahon shook his head. "I am an old dog," he said,

and as though the devil put the words in his mouth, he added: "I learned my tricks too long ago." Realizing what he had said and how it could be construed as mockery of his priesthood, he drank the cognac down like whisky and got up from the chair. His anger with himself, his situation, was too strong to conceal. But where to hide the darkness? He went to the bookshelf for want of any place to go except out the door. That was where he should have gone, but his feet would not take him there. "You are right, Nim. Things are so crazy," he said, looking at the books as though he was actually seeing them, and trying to ease matters for the others as well as for himself. "I coveted these books the first time I saw them."

It would have been easy for her to say, Take them, have them, and thus set off a round of banal protest to drown out the troubled moment, but neither she nor Rosenberg spoke. The conflict was his own, and they would not intervene to ease or to aggravate it. It was a kind of test of character, the ability to endure oneself in nakedness, and on her part, and perhaps Rosenberg's, to endure the nakedness of another's spirit. Whereas on his part, it had always been a matter of clothing quickly. The cloth . . . I can smell the cloth: the bartender in the homosexual bar. Phelan: he thought of him seeking the cloth, and he, the naked priest, all but urging it upon the man that he might clothe himself. He stood there, his back to the others, his hands in his pockets, and let it happen to him, whatever it was that was happening, the surfacing awareness that he had said what he had wanted to say, that there was no devil, only his own contention between will and want.

Finally he heard the clink of glass on glass and Rosenberg brought him the cognac. "Drink. It is the last of the bottle. But there is always a new bottle if a man wants to go out and get it."

McMahon, taking his hand from his pocket, drew with it the folded money Miss Chase had given him. He looked at it and then held it closer to the light to be sure: it was a hundred-dollar bill.

"Rosenberg," he said, taking the glass from the old man's hand, "where could you buy a piano for a hundred dollars?"

15

Nim waited for him in the church while McMahon returned to the rectory, changed his clothes, and made his excuses to Miss Lalor. The monsignor had been invited out to dinner and she hated to cook for the other two. She would give them eggs and set aside for the next night that night's menu. No family ever lived under such a matriarchy.

He found Nim walking up and down the side aisle, trying to see the stations of the cross, but the light was poor which, considering the artistic merits of the sculptures, was fortunate. An old Irish parishioner, half blind, was making the stations, her bones creaking at every genuflection. "Is it Father McMahon?" she said as he passed. "I could tell your step."

"How are you, Mrs. Carroll?"

"I've aches and pains," she whispered, "but otherwise I'm fine, thank God."

McMahon and Nim went out the side door where he had tried to catch up with her the day she first came to see him. On the street he repeated Mrs. Carroll's "Aches and pains but otherwise I'm fine, thank God."

"You know," Nim said, "I dig everything about religion except the church."

"And God," McMahon suggested.

"Sometimes I even dig him. But that's when things are pretty bad."

"Try it sometime when things are good. You'll like him better."

"Who needs him then?" she said.

They took a bus uptown to the warehouse off Broadway in the eighties where Rosenberg had called a friend. "Those old pianos you're always trying to get rid of, Michael," the pawnbroker had said with a wink to Nim and McMahon. "I have some young friends who might take one of them off your hands." And it had been arranged that the night watchman show them the dozen or so relics at the back of the storeroom.

The click of Nim's heels echoed through the huge loft. "People buying pianos today won't get the likes of these even on the installment plan," the watchman said, making the most of the chance to play salesman. "Of course, you have to have a house to suit them. They like more room than most."

He excused himself to turn on another light. A big man, on in years, he walked with a limp, and McMahon supposed he might have been a mover and incurred an injury.

Nim said, "Do you think everything in this place is alive to him? Did you hear, they like more room?"

"I hope they have life," McMahon said, thinking of all the classroom pianos in all the parochial schools in the city.

The watchman returned and they went on to where a row of bruised and battered uprights, some with keyboards open and some closed, stood against the wall.

"Look at them," the watchman said, "smiling up at you."

"The trouble is," McMahon said, "I'm not a dentist." He put his hand to one and struck a chord, or what would have been a chord when the old strings could make it.

"Some has more tune," the watchman admitted.

"So does the Liberty Bell." McMahon lifted the keyboard lid on the next one and tried it. The improvement in sound was slight, but the promise in each separate key as he struck it was greater. He stood back and looked at it in line with the others: it had the added advantage of being smaller.

"Maybe we should choose by the pound," Nim said.

"Believe me," McMahon said. He left the keyboard open and tried the others. None was better and some were worse. He borrowed the watchman's flashlight and examined the strings and mallets. Nim stood on tiptoe and looked in too. The wires were like ripples in a sea of dust. McMahon got down on the floor and tested the pedals by hand.

"You'd think it was a horse," the watchman said.

McMahon looked up at him. "Do you have a name for it too?"

"Dulcimer," the man said without hesitation. "It's a word I always liked. I wanted to call our daughter Dulcimer— you know, Dulcie for short? But the wife wouldn't have it. Sharon. It's a nice enough name."

"Now," McMahon said, getting up and dusting his hands and knees, "how do we get it from here to there?"

The watchman's face lengthened. "You've not arranged that?"

"There wasn't anything to arrange till now," McMahon said.

"True, true. What floor do you live on?"

"The fourth," Nim lied.

"The fifth," McMahon said.

"No elevator?"

"If I had an elevator I'd be buying on the installment plan," Nim said with asperity.

"Where do you live, Miss?"

She lifted her chin. "On Fifth Street near Avenue A."

"I was afraid it was San Francisco." The watchman took the weight off his feet, half-sitting on the closed board of the next piano. "We've got some black boys working for us who might moonlight it on Sunday if I can get hold of them. I'll phone from the office. But five floors. The young lady was right. I'll tell them four and you tell them the fifth."

"How much do you think it will cost?"

"The last time, fifteen dollars per man and twenty for the truck. Four men."

"Eighty dollars," McMahon said. Then: "Isn't there a bench or a stool goes with it?"

"No, sir. Them we can sell for money."

On the street again, the delivery arranged for Sunday

morning, McMahon said, "Now we have twenty dollars to spend on dinner. Where shall we go?"

"The Brittany," Nim said. "It's cheaper than most and I like it better. Do you know where it is?"

"Yes," McMahon said. Nothing more: it was within a few blocks of the rectory.

"Or better. There's a fish house on Third Avenue in the forties," Nim said, trying hard not to show her realization of why he had been reluctant about the Brittany.

"And we can have a drink at Tim Ryan's," he said. "He's an old friend of mine."

"And broadminded," Nim said.

McMahon did not answer.

"I'm sorry. Don't priests ever take girls to dinner?"

"You know the answer to that as well as I do, Nim. An agreement between us—no games?"

"No games," she repeated, and took his arm as they crossed the street toward Central Park. "But it is a game all the same, and I'm playing it even though I know I'm going to get hurt."

He was aware of her hand on his arm, more than aware. "Nobody's going to get hurt," he said.

"Let's just say nobody's going to cry. Will you go with me to see Professor Broglio?"

"I can't," McMahon said. "I have dress rehearsal in the morning for Sunday's concert."

"But by noon couldn't you get to Columbia?"

"I can try."

"Could I come to the concert Sunday?"

"It's in the school auditorium at three," he said. "I'll write you a pass. Otherwise it's two dollars."

"Two dollars!" Nim said, and then, "Forgive me."

"Toward the building fund."

Before walking through the park, Nim took off her shoes. "I'm quite primitive, you know."

"Savage," McMahon said, and then walking hand in hand, finding one another's hands by some mutual impulse he certainly was not going to examine then, they managed to throw off the gray mood that had come on them with the choosing of a restaurant. But McMahon could not take her to Tim Ryan's—for her sake, not his own. He could see the Irishman's cold blue eyes measuring the woman who consorted with off-duty priests. Broadminded Tim.

They drank where they ate, and it was better, the settling in to be themselves and with a waiter who calculated his tip by every drink and instead of hurrying, urged them to take their time—a public-private place.

Nim said: "If tomorrow you could go any place in the world you wanted to, where would it be?"

"Somewhere by the sea—with a long shore and no people anywhere. The sand would be damp and hard so I could run on it. I love to run. I had a dream once—it was as though I was chasing myself along a beach, trying to catch up."

"Did you?"

He shook his head.

"You love the sea and Stu hated it, except for the things beneath it. Protoplasmic man."

McMahon thought of the painting of Nim's, one that Wallenstein had admired, the last she had put away after he left. The undersea quality was in it. "You knew him well, Nim. Maybe better than you know."

"How do you mean?"

"That painting of yours, the one you asked if I liked?"

"It was the last thing I did while he was with me."

"I was just wondering if it might have had to do with his going away from you."

"I was becoming too much him to him, is that it?" she said after a moment.

"Or he was becoming too much you."

"I'd never have thought of it that way."

"Only in isolation would he have had what he needed of himself. I don't think you'll agree with this, but whatever he called it, I think he was looking for God." The thought of Phelan skimmed through his mind: something of this had come through to him too.

"Or the devil. Maybe he wanted to kill the devil, and I said he would shake hands with him."

"The world's infections," McMahon mused, "into the cauldron of his genius."

"Now that's spooky," Nim said. "When I told you that, that's the word I should have said, cauldron. It's the word he used, but I couldn't think of it. I said furnace. There are times you're very like him, Joe."

"There are times I even feel like him, whatever that means."

"I know what it means to me," Nim said. Her face, when he looked up, had become bleakly sad.

"Not tonight, not tonight," McMahon said. "I think we can manage a cognac. Then I've got to go home."

16

"It may seem wrong to you, but I do not feel grief for him, the way you tell his dying." He sat, a small man, deep in his chair and closed his eyes for a moment. His head was as bald as Picasso's. "Even when I knew him he lived on the edge of life, daring the step that might take him over. In a way it was me who brought him into the department. A mistake. Or was it? Who knows what is a mistake? Add up all the mistakes of my life and I am a success. Add up my successes and I am a failure. A man should not be in one place for thirty years. And if there is anything we can be sure about Tom Chase, he did not make that mistake. His name was a natural gift."

Nim said, "Professor Broglio, please tell us everything you can about him."

The old man grunted and scratched the top of his head. "Everything. Even that has a beginning. It was the first and last time I was ever political and I would say the same for him, the Adlai Stevenson campaign. It was in the old Marcantonio district, First Avenue on the edge of Harlem. We worked in an empty store, artists and writers for Stevenson. It was quite insane, ladies in mink, painters in dungarees, a classless society. Ha! All that does not matter but that's where we met. It was afterwards I got to know him, his rage at the frightened intellectuals, that was the time. Everybody playing it safe—afraid to think anything new, much less to teach it on the campuses. So I said, you are not afraid: teach. Teach what? What you know, how to paint, how to draw. He was a fine craftsman. And I got him a class a week to teach drawing, here where everything is new, experimental." He spoke ironically, hardly lifting his heavy-lidded eyes. He got up from the desk then, moving slowly with difficulty in straightening up at first, and McMahon thought he would have spent years in damp places to have become so arthritic. He moved a chair out of his way and took a picture down from the wall leaving a white space where it had hung. "I had forgotten this. It is his."

He brought it back and put it in Nim's hands. McMahon looked at it over her shoulder: a sketch of a market place such as he himself knew from the Italian section on Ninth Avenue—the stalls and baskets, and an aproned man putting something in the scale: a simple drawing of a complex scene, but the shape of the man told it all, the rhythm of his lifetime was in the line of his back.

"He did not sign it," Nim said.

"But it is his all the same."

"He must have had a body of painting," McMahon suggested, "for you to have been able to judge his work."

"I do not judge work, only how people go about it. Judgment I leave to my superiors. That is survival and he came to hate me for it. To answer your question, Father, there was a body of work. I took the head of the department to his place, a loft on Amsterdam Avenue, and the boss agreed. There was an opening that February. He was given the assignment on condition that he try to get a gallery and show within a year. Backwards, you say, but the boss had that kind of confidence in himself—and his contacts. Some painters are born, others are made."

"And was there a showing?" McMahon asked.

"Never to my knowledge. But his contract was renewed for a year. The serious students liked him. The others were in the majority, and before the year was out, he walked out on his contract. They were studying for credits, you see, and he did not approve of working in the arts for credit. He was hopeless, pursuing the absolute. Anarchy. And now you tell me what happened to him—and you, Miss Nim— what he was like when you knew him, and I repeat, hopeless. He was always running, even when he was standing still. But we did enjoy life together, wine . . . and women. We enjoyed, and that is the thing. Maybe it is the only thing." He reached out a gnarled hand and patted Nim's. "Do you know, Miss Nim, when your father brought you to see me, how long ago? . . ."

"Eight years," Nim said.

"I almost told you both about him then, what it is like to want everything so that you settle for nothing. But it was too complicated for me to try to explain in the presence of a scientist."

"A scientist," Nim said with a touch of derision.

"You are still at war with him," the old man said.

"No. It's an armed truce, if it's anything."

"But you are painting?" He turned her hand over and exposed the fingernails.

"Yes, thanks to him." She set the drawing on the desk.

"No. Thanks to yourself only. You may have the drawing."

"I do want it very much," she said.

"Then it is yours." He turned to McMahon. "Does she paint well, Father?"

"I think so. Do you know a man named Wallenstein?"

"I know the name very well. David Wallenstein is an important collector, mostly in the Impressionists."

"I think this man's name is Everett," McMahon said.

"That would be the son. A dilettante—so I have heard. I forget in what connection."

"He also collects—Tchelitchew among others."

"Ah, yes. There is a show, or was recently. Tchelitchew is not my dish."

"Mr. Wallenstein thinks I'm good," Nim said, with that characteristic thrust of the chin.

Broglio leaned back in his chair. "Who is to say a dilettante does not know? It is only himself he does not know."

McMahon asked: "Do you have the address where Chase had his loft, professor?"

While the old man got a ragged address book from the

bottom drawer of his desk and groped its pages, Nim said: "Was there anyone else, professor—anyone who might have known him later?"

He wrote the address in a painfully neat, almost exquisite script, and writing it, seemed to ignore her question. He gave the card to McMahon. Then he said, "Is it that important to you, Miss Nim?"

"Yes."

He drew a deep breath and let it out in a sigh. "The truth brings its own kind of pain—to teller and listener. Yes, my dear, there was someone else, a woman by the name of Andrea Robinson, and I ought to tell you, her husband was a trustee of the university, a connection not unimportant to my protégé—and myself."

Nim took it face on, not so much as flinching at the name, Robinson, by which she had known the man. "Mrs. what Robinson, professor?"

"Mrs. Alexander Brewer Robinson, and I would think the address is still Park Avenue."

Afterwards they sat, Nim and McMahon, on a bench and looked down from Morningside Heights. Neither of them had anything to say for some time. "Well," Nim said finally, "I do like that touch, Stuart Robinson—where his mind went when he made up a name to give me. It gives things a kind of continuity. This one I shall take on myself, Joe. Andrea Robinson, Park Avenue." She looked at the sketch. "I've just realized: Miss Chase would probably pay five hundred dollars for this. Did you see *The Times* this morning?"

"No."

"I must say the story brightened up the obituary page."

McMahon took the card Broglio had given him from his pocket. "I've got to get back," he said, "but I'll go down by way of Amsterdam Avenue."

"Confessions, visits to the sick, things like that?"

"Yes."

"Then I'll see you tomorrow," Nim said, much too brightly for the way he knew she felt. "Good luck with the concert."

McMahon left her sitting on the stone bench. He looked back before he turned the corner, but she was not watching him. She was staring out over Harlem, her elbow on her knee, her chin in her hand, the framed drawing under her arm. He stood for a moment looking at her, and thought that this was how it was going to be, as though every parting might be the last.

The address on Amsterdam Avenue had long since become a number in a vast red brick housing complex.

17

Phelan, propped up on pillows, the bed slightly elevated, his hands folded on the white sheet looked serene as a saint who had banished his demons, a picture, McMahon realized, out of romantic, holy-card lore. Neither saint nor sinner was free of demons so long as he was mortal. All of El Greco's saints were tortured men, the fugue of the artist's violence on himself.

McMahon stood a moment, reluctant to waken the man, and thought of Broglio's comments on Muller-Chase. He was wrong about him, however right he had made it sound. He had thought at the time, watching the painfully exquisite hand in which the professor had written the Amsterdam address, this old man has exhausted himself in perfectionism, but he has perfected the wrong things: he is half-blind, having never looked into the sun. Muller might have blinded himself, but he had looked it in the face.

Phelan opened his eyes. "I wondered if you'd given me up to Dr. Connelly, Father."

"I've been busy," McMahon said. It had taken an act of will for him to have come that afternoon at all.

"Well, I'm going home tomorrow," Phelan said without enthusiasm.

"Good. What happened to your neighbor?" The other bed was empty, stripped, the fresh linens in a heap, yet to be spread.

"They went out of here like an Easter procession. Father, if I was given my choice, I'd like to be like them. They came and kissed me good-bye, all of them, the children, the women, even the uncle. A lifetime couldn't have made us closer, and you know, I started out hating every mortal one of them—noisy, busy, and so damned happy. About what? Life, I guess. And I said to myself, Dan, my boy, these are God's children—the way he made them, and if you want to be God's deputy, you'd better find out what they're about."

McMahon, troubled at the ease with which he had allowed himself to be drawn into Phelan's fantasy of the priestly life—using the situation to compensate the Lord for his own backsliding—wanted to break in on the reverie. But that, he felt, would also be a kind of wickedness. He listened him out.

"Like a miraculous conversion, I was with them. Like a hand lifted a veil from my eyes. The hand of God?" He thought about it for a second or two. "Or was it just the police finally going away? Or me seeing Dr. Connelly... I don't know whether I like him or not."

McMahon was glad to get on the subject of Dr. Connelly. "You've only see him what—twice?"

Phelan nodded. "It's important that I do like him though, isn't it?"

"You have to get through to one another. It won't be as easy as it was with your neighbors." McMahon indicated the empty bed.

"My neighbors," Phelan repeated thoughtfully. "I'm going home a different man than I came. Another thing—Pedrito Morales came in to see me yesterday. He said it was his fault, what I did." Phelan laughed. "A Puerto Rican heart— pride, temper, honor. You might say I am now an honorary Puerto Rican. And Lord, how I hated those people until this fiasco. He apologized for what happened that night in his house. And I've been thinking, Father—what it takes to gain respect. A knife or a gun. It isn't right."

"We've all got violence in us, Dan. It depends on what we do with it." And he told Phelan what Muller had said of the artist's violence.

Phelan grinned. "That's great, you know. Really great.

Remember one of the first things I said when you came to see me—I thought he was a holy man? I'm not as stupid as I thought I was. Or even as crooked inside." He didn't say anything for a minute. "They don't know yet who killed him?"

"No."

"Funny, young Morales coming here. Maybe they think I killed him—which, in a crazy way, is what I wanted them to think when I pulled out the knife upstairs. Priscilla knew it. How I've hated her for seeing through me all these years. No, I've hated myself for what she saw."

"For what you thought she saw," McMahon suggested.

"All right. For what *I* saw."

"Did you tell that to Dr. Connelly?"

"Something like it. Understandable, he said. To him, everything is understandable. That's what scares me. I'd rather go to confession."

"And tell as sins the things you don't understand?"

"That's what you're for, Father. Whose sin you shall forgive, they are forgiven. Whose sins you shall retain, they are retained."

"Dan, it's not that simple being a priest today. Three Our Fathers and three Hail Marys and pray to the Holy Spirit just won't do any more."

"I'm a Holy Ghost man myself," Phelan said, again with a smile.

"I'd like to be myself, sometimes. But that's a copout. The young people want to know what is sin and why, and the answer that the Church says so is not enough. It's not even enough for me in my own confession."

"It's enough for me," Phelan said.

"Then you'd better do some more thinking about this change you want to make in your life."

"What I'd like you to do for me, Father—it's asking a lot but I'm going to ask it: go and see Priscilla and tell her what we've been talking about, that you think maybe I have a vocation . . . something like that."

"I didn't say I thought you had a religious vocation. I

don't know whether you do or not, and I don't think you know it yourself."

"Tell her something!" Phelan's agitation was sudden, and it revealed the instability, the fear beneath the dream of serenity. In a word, he was a desperate man.

"Are you afraid to go home, Dan?"

"Yes!"

"You're still a sick man. She won't make any demands on you."

"You know all about those demands, don't you, Father? You could give her advice on how to get me into bed. One more expert on how to fix a marriage. I don't want it fixed!"

"Easy, Dan . . . there's time, and there's Dr. Connelly. I'll tell her about him if you want me to."

"I'll get out of here," Phelan said, "and I'll run, believe me, I'll run, and the cops will bring me down then for sure. And there'll be one nice clean thing about it that way— you can give me a Christian burial."

McMahon, heavy with helplessness, said, "I'll go and see her tonight. What time do you go home tomorrow?"

"By eleven-thirty. That's check-out time. Or check-in time, whatever way you look at it."

"I'll be here if I can and go home with you."

"Morales said he'd borrow a car."

"I'll check up on the arrangements tonight, Dan. Just rest and make your plans the way you think you want them now. A few prayers may help."

"I know one thing I'll pray for—just that they don't make any goddamned fiesta over me coming home."

Miss Lalor had all her priests home to supper that night, amiable as a hen with chicks even if she had never laid an egg. And McMahon had been wrong about the menu: he had forgotten it was Saturday night. By way of her pattern of association, Irish with Boston, and Boston with custom, and the custom of baked beans on Saturday night, she had made it her own tradition. Even the monsignor could not change it, and no longer tried, for it was no longer a matter that troubled him. But the other priests: what was more painful than sitting cramped with gas in the confessional box? McMahon ate bread and butter. Food no longer interested him anyway.

Phelan had rightly anticipated the fiesta plans for his homecoming. The women were hanging balloons and pinning flowers of papier maché to the curtains. The amplified guitar was going strong again, vibrating through the building. Happiness was a loud noise. McMahon had a glass of beer with the women, and then managed with no great grace to tell Priscilla Phelan that he wanted to talk with her. He suggested the room she had given Muller.

"I rented it today," she said.

She did not want to talk with him, McMahon realized. She was living her own kind of fantasy. But he had promised Phelan. "I'll come back a little later." He asked Mrs. Morales if Pedrito was home. He was and so, a week to the day later, McMahon climbed the dim, ill-smelling stairway again.

Pedrito and his friends were at the kitchen table, also drinking beer. A deck of cards lay in an untidy heap where they had wearied of the game. One of the boys was on the phone trying to reach a girl named Felicita. McMahon declined a beer but took the chair that had been vacated by the boy on the telephone.

"So you're going to bring Mr. Phelan home tomorrow, Pedrito. What time?"

Pedrito shrugged. "I got the car all morning."

"Make it eleven and I'll come with you."

"If I was him I would not come home," Pedrito said.

"Why?"

"She's got a pig in the back room."

McMahon was a few seconds figuring out what he meant. "A policeman?"

"That's how we see him, Father."

"How does Mrs. Phelan see him?"

"Ask her." Pedrito kept his eyes down. He picked up

one of the cards and flicked its edge with his thumb, a snapping sound. "We don't like pigs in the house."

The boy on the phone said, "Felicita! It's me, Marcelo." To the others he said, "I got her! Hey, I got her!"

"So. It ain't television, ask her about the other girls. How many?" This from the boy at the end of the table.

"Shut up," Pedrito said to him. But he got up from the table and jerked his head to the priest to follow him. They went into the next room where the effigy of Muller had been laid out. "See, Father, the poor bastard—the cops keep pushing him around, and *zook!* next time for real." Pedrito pantomimed the thrust of a knife into his own heart.

McMahon glanced at the picture of the Sacred Heart, the shiny drops of blood. "How do you know he's a cop?"

"It figures, that's all. He looks like one."

"Pedrito, maybe it's none of our business. If Dan doesn't have anything to hide, maybe he'd like the idea of someone living there. He didn't kick Muller out, did he?"

Pedrito thought about it. "I think I get what you say, Father. But what if he's got something to hide? Somebody? The cops know better, he don't use a knife on Muller, not him."

"That isn't our business either, Pedrito."

"My friend's business, Father, that's my business. I never liked him, but he got guts, and pride and honor. I don't like to see him hurt any more."

"Eleven at the hospital," McMahon said.

"And I don't like pigs no more than they like me," the boy said over the banister.

McMahon went down the stairs, his head throbbing with weariness, with too much confinement in too small places, the smell of breaths, of bodies, of waste, and with almost the taste in his mouth of the little lusts of man. Every year he had gone home for a few days after the concert, but this year he would not go home. His mother had died and the house was sold. But he longed to breathe clean air and find God in the skies, to push out the walls of the tabernacle where men called priests had boxed their Savior in like a butterfly. And stifled him? The God-is-dead school was also dead. But Fair House of Joy, where was it? He tried to track the association, and it went straight back to Nim and the songs of Kathleen Ferrier, and how Muller had linked them in his mind. And tomorrow *The Bells*. And the next day, and the next?

Mrs. Phelan left the women and went out on the stoop with him. She sat on the parapet. "Look, Father, you've been very kind. But I think I can handle matters from here."

Another mind your own business, McMahon thought. "I wanted to tell you about Dr. Connelly."

"I know all about him."

"Dan ought to keep on seeing him, even if it's expensive."

"For what?"

"He can help him with a lot of his problems."

She lit a cigarette. "I thought you told me I could do that. All those sessions we had, Father?"

McMahon felt his temper rise under her sarcasm. "A priest can be wrong. I should have recommended a separation then, but I didn't."

"But now you do. Is that it, Father?"

"That's up to Dr. Connelly."

"No, Father. Dan doesn't want him and neither do I. Dan's my husband and I can take care of him."

"All right . . . your husband, Mrs. Phelan, but not your child. Dan's got to have a chance to stand on his own feet."

"Father, I've never said this to a priest before. Thanks for everything, but go to hell."

18

It was a clear and sparkling day, that Sunday in New York, when even windows that were not washed looked as though they had been. The streets looked cleaner, and somehow there was more sky. Father McMahon did not go to the hospital: he could not, for the monsignor was not feeling well and asked McMahon to sing the high Mass at eleven-thirty. McMahon welcomed it as an act of God, lifting him out of the slough of despair. Afterwards he walked to the river and back and then fixed his own breakfast in the kitchen. He was hungrier than he had thought he would be, and felt unburdened, almost as though his failure with the Phelans had humbled him in a way that was pleasing to God. It remained now for some enlightenment to come upon him in the freshness of his spirit. And for that he offered up the afternoon's concert.

The monsignor managed to rise from his sickbed and Miss Lalor wore her Easter hat. Half the parish turned out, and neighborhood people who, having been persuaded to buy tickets, used them. Considering the fact that he and his girls were playing opposite the first Met double-header of the season, McMahon accepted the number of men in the audience as a tribute—to the girls. He did not look for Nim; he avoided looking toward the reserved-seat section. The girls, dressed in white, convened in the back of the auditorium. He could hear the clack of Sister Justine's frog over the murmur of conversation and shuffling of feet and creaking of seats. At three o'clock sharp he went onstage from the wings, and one hand on the piano from which he would conduct, he bowed, a curt, formal nod, and sat down before the keyboard. Both his hands and his knees were trembling and he wished profoundly that the whole thing was over. But that was not so either: he merely wished to be lost in the music, the self submerged, sublimated, and therefore exalted. He marched the chorus in to "Pomp and Circumstance" which he disliked but which they loved, and it was they who were going to make the music of the day.

And make music they did. To be sure, there was a mistake here and there, but only the trained ear caught it, and the joy of young voices singing burst over everyone like the soaring of spring itself. The audience clapped and stamped, and Father McMahon crossed the stage and led the soloists to the front. He shook hands with each of them, and then to both his delight and embarrassment, little Marietta Hernandez stood on tiptoe and kissed his cheek.

He went back to the piano and without a signal to anyone began to play "Bell Bottom Rock." The girls caught on at once and went into their thing, that uninhibited rhythm, each her own, the jerk and the halt and the shoulder shakes, with the little buds of bosoms popping up like buttons. Over his shoulder, the back of his head to the audience, he said to Sister Justine where she stood in the wings, "Curtain!"

And on that wild improvisation, the curtains closed.

People flocked around him in the basketball court afterwards, so many people, good, warm people all. Only then did he allow himself to search the faces for Nim's. The flash of her smile when he saw her gave him a stab of pleasure. He worked his way unhurriedly toward her, greeting, accepting the praise of everyone who stopped him on the way. Nim wore a green suit with an orange scarf at the throat.

"It was great," she said, extending her hand, "really the most."

He shook her hand briefly. Even gloves, he noticed. "It was a lot." The words had become a kind of theme between them. He introduced her to the other people who came up, to Mrs. Morales who was so proud of her two girls.

"Where's Carlos?" McMahon asked.

"Home. He wiggle . . . like the girls, you know at the end?" Mrs. Morales covered her good teeth in self-conscious laughter.

"You liked that part, did you?"

Mrs. Morales rolled her eyes and sidled away from them.

"Now I know what it's all about," Nim said.

"Did the piano come?"

"It certainly did. Now that *was* a lot. Doors came off hinges. People came out I'd never seen before. Words came out I'd never heard before."

"Where did you put it?"

"In the icebox," Nim said, and he laughed, the ridiculous image somehow appropriate. "Against the wall to the kitchen," she said then. "In winter it's warmer there and not so damp."

People were leaving them alone now. "You ought to go," Nim said.

"We're merely talking."

"I know, but they want you too."

"What about the Robinson woman?"

"I called her. Very Park Avenue: 'Oh, yes, darling. I knew him well. Do come and see me.' Joe—Father," she quickly amended, "I can't go alone. I thought I could. She invited me for cocktails and I asked if I could bring a friend."

"When?"

"Today—after five."

"Let's go then," McMahon said. "Free drinks for artists and the clergy. Why not?"

"It was presumptuous of me," Nim said.

McMahon said, "No games. Remember?"

Nim nodded.

He looked at his watch. "Five-thirty in front of the Metropolitan Museum."

McMahon wore his sport jacket and slacks and his black sweater. He did not have much of a wardrobe altogether, and little need until now for more than he had. On impulse, he put on the beads the flower child had given him in the Village. He took them off again and put them in his pocket until he got out of the house.

"Have a good time," the monsignor said as he went through the hall. "You've earned it, Joseph." When he had almost reached the door, the old man called him back to the office. "Are you planning to go up home this spring?"

"I hadn't thought much about it, Monsignor."

"Well, let me know. There's other places you could go. Mind, I'm not trying to get rid of you, but sometimes I have the feeling, Joseph, you'd like to be rid of us for a while."

"It's the spring, Monsignor, and I'm a little tired. That's all."

"Suit yourself, suit yourself." The old man went back to the ledger open on the desk. It was auditing time and McMahon understood the pastor's clinging to his bed that morning. He wished the vacation had not been mentioned, the fantasies it started in his mind: a few days' freedom and three dollars and eighty cents in his pocket. But then the monsignor always gave him a generous gift out of the concert money.

Other guests were arriving at the Park Avenue address at the same time as Nim and McMahon, and within the building—what in the old days was called a town house— a very large party was in progress. The maid taking wraps suggested the elevator although a marble staircase ascended to where most of the people were: laughter and the cadence of many voices and the tinkling sound of expensive glass. Some of the guests wore evening clothes.

"What have you got us into?" McMahon said, steering Nim toward the staircase.

"I'll say this for Stu: no rags to riches for him. No, man. Riches to rags. I'm scared. I don't know why, but I'm scared."

"That's why I'm here," McMahon said. "Hansel and Gretel."

"Ugh," Nim said.

"No. Humperdinck."

Nim made a face, but they too were able to arrive smiling at the balcony beyond which was the great living room where, as Nim said, Mrs. Robinson was having a few friends in to cocktails. People were gathered in clusters in the soft, sparkling light of the chandeliers, all making the sounds of the very rich, McMahon thought. There was not a guffaw in the house. It was like walking onto a motion-picture set, not that he had ever done that either, but it was the unreality of the genuine thing, nature imitating art. A waiter came up to them with champagne.

Nim took a glass, but McMahon said, "I wonder if I might have Scotch instead?"

"Yes, sir."

"Savoir-faire," Nim murmured. "I wonder how we find our hostess."

"We may never find her," McMahon said, "and you know, it has just occurred to me, you could make a way of life out of this, just walking in on parties with the invited guests."

"It's been done," Nim said. "Here comes somebody. Stay with me, Joe."

The woman came, dark-haired and tall, with a kind of angular poise to her gait. She was sleek in black silk, shoulders bare and bare-V'd to the navel with bell-legged trousers that swished as she walked. She put her glass in the hand with the cigarette and offered Nim her free one. "I'm Andrea Robinson," she said.

"Nim Lavery. And this is my friend, Joseph McMahon."

"You are nice," the woman said, giving him her hand as well as her long-lashed eyes. "Are you a painter? Do I know you?"

"Miss Lavery is the painter," McMahon said.

"And you don't know me either," Nim said, almost belligerently. Then, in retreat: "I thought we could talk — when you said to come today. I didn't know . . ."

"But we can talk, my dear. When you called it seemed like a voice from the dead. Which in a way it is, isn't it? What I mean to say, I was always insisting that Tom come to things like this—my perversity, for he loathed them. I wanted the fact established that I had a world of my own, and he could not have cared less."

McMahon was disconcerted at the ease with which she slipped into intimacy. As though it were a negligée. He was glad to see the waiter return with a bottle of Chivas Regal, a glass with ice and a bottle of soda on the tray.

"Just the ice," McMahon said, and he let the man half-fill the glass with whisky.

"When was it that you and he were friends?" the Robinson woman asked Nim.

"Last year and the year before."

"Were they good years for him?"

"I think so," Nim said.

The woman smiled, showing the lines in her face that were concealed most of the time. "I'm sure they were." She touched Nim's arm with her fingertips, and McMahon for the first time could see Muller-Chase's attraction to her. "And were they good years for you?"

"The best," Nim said.

"Then I'm glad for you—and I suppose for all his women, now that he is gone."

"There's only one question really, Mrs. Robinson," Nim said. "Do you know where his paintings are?"

"I would have asked you the same thing. It's eight years since I last saw him. His loft was as bare as the steppes of Asia, all of his canvases crated. I asked him where they were going. To the bottom of the Atlantic Ocean. You do that, I said, and I'll jump in after them. But you can jump in and out of things so easily, Andrea, he said. and I think I knew then that I would not see him any more."

"Did you?" McMahon asked.

"Not ever. But I understand now I must have barely missed him at a gallery opening two weeks ago. Or did I see him and not recognize the beard? I have the feeling I did. And I can't help wondering if seeing me, he didn't duck out. I don't suppose we'll ever know now and I'm glad. You can't go home again. Maybe I wasn't home to him, but I was something for a few years." She became flippant again. "It's like a French novel, isn't it, mistresses comparing notes?"

A tall man came up behind her, too young to be her husband, McMahon thought. Or too young to be a trustee of a university. He kissed the back of her neck. She whirled around, welcoming the touch even before she knew whose it was. "Chet, how nice that you could come." To Nim and McMahon she said, "Darlings, do go in. I'll come soon and introduce you."

She drifted from them, taking the young man whom she had not introduced with her by the hand to greet more people emerging from the elevator.

"Let's go," Nim said.

"No. Let's see it through," McMahon said.

"There isn't anything to see through. Not that I want to look at any more. I'm not as brave as I thought I was." She moved toward the stairs, but the newly arriving guests blocked her way.

"Nim, are you afraid we might meet Wallenstein again?"

"Yes."

"And you don't want him to think you're chasing after him. You don't want to have to remind him of his promise."

"It wasn't a promise."

"It's the only kind of promise these people make, you silly girl."

"It's all so . . . decadent," Nim said.

"Don't you remember—that's what you liked about his house when we were there."

"But this is so much more. And I was hurt, her talking that way about Stu." She looked up at McMahon. "You like it here, don't you?"

"I like the booze," he said. His glass was almost empty.

"It isn't only that."

"And I want to know."

Nim finished her champagne and before she could find a place to put the glass a waiter came and replenished it.

"I like this too," she said, "but one shouldn't get too fond of it."

"You sound like Lee at the Battle of Fredericksburg."

They found a corner for themselves in the living room, a corner lined with books, leather-bound classics, uncut, McMahon suspected, and then contemplated himself for a moment, this habit of supporting his own morale by criticizing the mores of the rich.

"You're always surprising me, the things you know," Nim said.

"Like what?"

"The Battle of Fredericksburg."

"I'm a kind of fraud," he said, "making the most of bits and pieces. That I know, for example, because Lee actually said it of the Battle of Marye's Heights where the Irish Brigade was decimated. Charge after charge—absolutely pointless. They had no hope of taking the Heights. Utter madness. That was when Lee is supposed to have said, 'It's fortunate that war's so terrible. We might become too fond of it.'"

McMahon had become aware while talking of a gray-bearded man edging his way toward them away from the group he had been with. "What Lee said was—if you'll forgive the intrusion—'It is well that war is so terrible, or we should grow too fond of it.' I'm Jacob Burke. I'm a Civil War buff and I overheard. You don't mind?"

"No." McMahon introduced himself and Nim.

"What do you think Meagher had in mind? I'm pretty sure it was Meagher that led the charge."

"Thomas Francis Meagher," McMahon said. "One of the Young Ireland emigrés of 1848. And I would think he had in mind proving that the Irish were not cowards. They'd had a rotten war record, as you know."

"Yes, yes, and they had reason—the inequity of the draft and all that. Not quite the same today, but something to the comparison. But you see, the question I ask: was it not simply that Meagher was a bad general? Pride, of course, but a bad field officer. And then I suggest, it's what you've done with history—McMahon, you say—your inverted Irish pride that takes satisfaction in that debacle. The lost cause mystique, hopeless heroism."

"You may have something," McMahon said. "The reason I happen to know the story: it's a legend the old soldiers tell whenever the Sixty-Ninth Division gets together."

"It's a great pity there are old soldiers left to perpetuate such legends," Burke said. "That's how they make young soldiers." And with that he nodded formally and went back to his own group.

"Now him I dig," Nim said.

"I'm sure there are others if we just charge in," McMahon said.

"Remember the Irish at Marye's Heights."

If he got a little drunk it would be very easy, McMahon thought. But he did not want to do that. He wanted to know more about their hostess because the fact had emerged that she was the first person they had come on from Muller-Chase's past who might have seen him within a week of his death. He thought about Rosenberg's note on the Tchelitchew affair, Muller's: a man should not run from the devil. He should open his arms.

"Nim, can you see your friend Stu in this room?"

"You're psychic—or intuitive maybe. Something. That's what I was trying to do right now. He'd be going around, his hands behind his back, making faces at all the portraits on the wall. Then he'd go off through the house looking for young people. There aren't any."

"We haven't looked through the house," McMahon said.

"I suppose we could," Nim said tentatively.

"Wait till I get a refill." There was a circular bar in the middle of the room.

When he returned, Nim said, "What are we looking for?"

"I don't know exactly."

"She could have seen him at the opening. Is that it?"

"That's it."

"Did she go to it to look for him? I might have, you know. Sometimes I think I wanted to, but I was too proud

to look for him. She'd have known his hangup on Tchelitchew."

"Let's just look and listen," McMahon said.

"Stop, look and listen," Nim said. "Or maybe just look,
listen and stop. Maybe that's best."

McMahon said, "When I was going to high school I used
to race a train to the crossing every morning. If I didn't
make it ahead of the train I was late for first class."

"If you hadn't made it, I should think you'd've been late
for the last class also," she said.

McMahon laughed.

"Did you always want to be a priest?"

"No. Just most of the time."

"Where did you grow up?"

"Upstate—near Albany."

"Family?"

"Father and mother, both dead now. Two sisters—one
in Boston married to a doctor. One a nun."

"What did your father do?"

"He worked on the New York Central, a conductor."

"Working class. I like that," Nim said.

"I think you've said that before—working class and the
filthy rich."

"So today I have the best of two worlds."

On the steps they met Mrs. Robinson. "You're not going
so soon? We haven't really talked at all."

What she meant, McMahon felt, was that she intended
them to go now. He sensed a subtle imperative. He chanced
then a gambit that implied an intimate knowledge of her
circle. "I thought maybe Mr. Wallenstein might be here."

"I thought so too. Not even a RSVP, which isn't like
him. But it is really. Everything bores him."

"Except Tchelitchew," McMahon said.

Did she tense a little at the name? He could not be sure.
"He must bore him too now, for Wally to sell off the drawings."

"Did Wallenstein know Chase?"

This time her reaction was direct: "Are you a policeman, Mr. McMahon?"

"Good God, no. But I'd better watch that. I sound like one, don't I? I'm a musician." He had said too much and carried the whole thing off badly and he knew it.

"I don't mind the police," Mrs. Robinson said, "but I do like to see their identification." She gathered the folds of her silken trousers. "It's been so nice meeting you both." She swept past them.

"Let's go," Nim said.

"I guess we'd better after that."

At the foot of the stairs they met someone McMahon had not expected to meet, Brogan, and another detective, giving their hats to the maid. Brogan arched his eyebrows and looked from McMahon to Nim and then back at the priest again. "It's a small world."

"Isn't it?" McMahon murmured.

"Do you know Father McMahon? Detective Tomasino." Brogan contracted his introduction.

McMahon had no choice but to introduce Nim to them both.

"Miss Lavery," Brogan said. "Mrs. Robinson told me on the phone that you'd be here. It's just Father McMahon I didn't expect."

It had had to come sooner or later, McMahon realized. So did Nim, for she said: "It was I who went to Father McMahon. I thought the man he found might have been someone I'd known."

"Father was a good one to go to," Brogan said easily, "if you weren't going to come to the police." He intercepted the maid and asked her if there was a place they could talk by themselves.

She led them to a room beneath the staircase, the library. "Will I bring you cocktails, sir?"

"That'd be grand," Brogan said, having caught the lilt in her voice. "Bourbon for me and my partner. Scotch for Father, and the young lady?"

Nim shook her head.

Brogan tried hard to play the comfortable host. "Sit down, sit down. That set the Irish lass back a bit, me calling you Father."

"If she's never set back more," McMahon said, "she'll bear up under the shock."

"Why didn't you come to the police, miss?"

"I had nothing to tell you."

"You could've told us his name."

"I didn't know his real name either. Not then."

Brogan turned to the priest. "Father, you don't mind me asking, what are you doing here?"

"We were trying to find out if Chase left any paintings. Just trying to find out."

"Did you?"

"It begins to look as though he destroyed them all."

"If there ever were any. I have a feeling we'd know it by now after that piece in yesterday's paper. I'm no great authority, but it seems to me if somebody paints a picture, he wants people to see it. For Christ's sake, when I was a kid I took home every chimney I ever made smoke come out of. My mother's still got one of them hanging in the kitchen."

Nim laughed. So did McMahon. Brogan was human again. To McMahon he said: "Is this the girl—the name you mentioned in your statement?"

"Nim," McMahon said.

"What I'd like you to do, miss, come into the station house tomorrow morning and give us a statement—where you met him, where you saw him last, just the facts. That way, you're checked out, and Tommy here and I have done our job. It's not like we spend all our time on this case, you know. We've had four more homicides in the precinct since. And I've still got the notion we know where our man is."

"Phelan?"

"I'm not saying a thing, Father."

"Sorry."

"No offense taken. But I ought to tell you, we know you

were at Columbia University yesterday too. Just don't try to do our work for us. Now here come the drinks, so let's relax and enjoy them." Before the maid left he asked her to send Mrs. Robinson in.

Nim and McMahon exchanged glances. "I don't want to see her again," Nim said, not minding that the detectives heard it.

"It will take her a while with that crowd," Brogan said. "Let Father have his drink. You must have gone over that gallery list pretty close to wind up here."

"No. We came by way of the university. Miss Lavery knew a professor there who had known both Chase and Mrs. Robinson." McMahon was aware of what he was doing: trying to give their hostess her own back for having mentioned Nim to the police.

Brogan took out his notebook and pencil. "The professor's name?"

Nim spelled the name for him.

"You one-upped us there, Father. We came dead-end in a housing development on Amsterdam Avenue. Any other leads you can give us?"

"No. We're not looking for leads," McMahon said.

"We're trying to get hold of your friend Wallenstein again, by the way. But he's gone off to some island in Maine. Drummond Island. Ever hear of it, Miss Lavery?"

Nim shook her head. "Could we go now?"

McMahon drank down most of the drink.

Brogan went to the door with them. "Keep in touch," he said to the priest, and then to Nim: "Don't forget tomorrow morning, Miss Lavery."

When they reached the street Nim said, "Why did you tell her you were a musician?"

McMahon buttoned his jacket. A wind was rising. And he did not want to give her the answer which he gave nonetheless: "I guess I had in mind to avoid scandal."

"That's how I figured it." She turned one way and then the other to get her bearings. "I think I'll take the Lexington subway. Thank you for coming here with me—for the concert—everything."

"We'll both take the Lexington subway," McMahon said. "I want to see that piano in its natural habitat."

Nim was able to smile again. "To hell with Mrs. Robinson. Right?"

"Right."

There was a feeling of exquisite pain to that subway ride: it was for McMahon like going forward and backward in time at once, fragments of memory and ploys into the unknown which yet was deeply known, felt, instinctual knowing . . . his mother's wake, his sister's vows, Nim at the sacristy door, that moment among the Orthodox icons, his own prostration, the anointing of his fingers, the first trembling elevation of the Host and the terror that he would drop it . . . as though Christ had not fallen thrice himself on the road to Calvary. Whatever else drink did for him, it clarified his images and made him tell himself the truth: conscience and longing, Joseph, the spirit and the flesh. He and Nim did not talk: just awareness, and to him, every face in that subway car was marked with the condition of mortality: choices made for peace or for the promise of peace or for the abandonment of peace in the abandonment of promise.

They came up from underground at Astor Place into a virtual star of possible directions. On Sunday there were not many people, mostly students from NYU, heading back to their digs, and a few stray drunks cast up from the Bowery. Following Nim's lead, they walked past the old Cooper Union. His grandfather had gone there to classes soon after he arrived from Ireland. He thought of his mother again: how when things turned out badly she would say, "Man proposes, God disposes." Which was wrong: it was the other way around.

"Do you like pizza?" Nim said.

"Yes." Pizza was a very good thing to think about at the moment.

"Pizza with sausage?"

"Yes."

"Or anchovy?"

"Sausage."

Actually he did not care much for either pizza or sausage.

But carrying the box up the long flight of stairs a few minutes later, he breathed deeply of the pie's fragrance. Nim turned on the lights. "I don't have window shades," she said. "No neighbors up this high, unless they use a telescope. Besides, I need all the morning light I can get. I get up at six, you know, and work till ten."

"I get up at six most mornings," McMahon said, "but I don't quite like it."

"You would if your work was going well. Put the pie in the kitchen. There's a light switch just inside the door."

They were strangers, McMahon thought. He was in an alien world. He snapped on the light and caught sight of a cockroach just before it disappeared beneath the stove. He put the pie down carefully in the center of the white-topped table.

Nim had brought a lamp and set it next to the piano. "Beautiful," he said. The old wood had been brought up to a high gloss, its scars stained out. He could smell the furniture polish.

"I'm afraid to get it tuned," she said. "This way I don't seem to play so badly."

McMahon lifted the lid and struck a chord, the notes going off in all directions. "This way I don't play so goodly," he said.

Nim's eyes caught his and held them. "I want to say this, Joe. It's all right, your being here. I don't expect anything of you—just talk and company."

He held his arms out to her and she rushed into them. "Talk and company," he said at her ear, holding her close against him. She would be standing on tiptoe.

"I said expect, I didn't say want."

Such lies we tell to prime the truth, he thought, and then thought no more, just holding her tightly, kissing her hair, then her forehead, her cheek, her lips. The moment of self-repossession came when, to balance herself, Nim reached out and by inadvertence touched the piano keys. They drew apart and after a moment, McMahon said, "We've imported a chaperon."

Nim looked down at the piano and struck one note, then another. She gathered her fingers into a fist and sprung them open again. "Of all the things I didn't need—was to get hung up on a priest."

"What about the priest?"

"Yes. What about him? I want to know. I have a thousand questions." She walked away from him, hugging herself. "Please, turn on the electric heater. It's cold in here and I want to be comfortable. I want to talk. I want you to talk. I'm twenty-nine years old, and I know quite a lot—about men, about a lot of things. Have you ever been with a woman?"

"Yes. But..." He couldn't say it.

She said it for him. "I know. The other women weren't like me. What's his name... Tim Ryan's place?"

McMahon went to the small space heater in the middle of the room, a string of extension cords linking it to the wall outlet. He snapped it on and, squatting, watched the gradual rise of the orange glow.

Nim changed her suit jacket for a pullover sweater. She came and stood beside him. "And afterwards, what?"

"Guilt. An agony of guilt, confession, penance, starting over."

"Starting over what?"

"Trying to live up to my vow. Prayer, work, more work, walking, walking, music... and trying to keep Christ alive in me."

"Whatever that means," Nim said. She lit a cigarette and sat down on the floor, cross-legged, near the heater.

"It means..." He went to the daybed and sat on the corner of it, groping his mind for something she would not put down out of hand. "It means trying to be His representative on earth, to teach, to help people live decent lives, to encourage them when they fail, to assure them of forgiveness . . ." It sounded so hollow to him, so thin against the monstrous clamor of his own heartbeat.

"It's playing Christ," she said, "it's forgiving sin and jangling the keys to heaven. I'm not making fun of it, Joe. I know what it's like to get rid of guilt, to hurt somebody and then make up for it. And I think I dig what it means to kneel in church and say, 'God, I need you.' And if a man comes down from the altar and says, 'Go in peace,' and I know he's a good man, I'll go in peace . . . I think. In other words, I'm trying to say I know what a priest is to people who believe in priests. But what is he to himself?"

It was a question he had not been able to ask himself. A priest should be nothing to himself, God's mirror . . . bump, bump, bump. "A vessel, a vehicle . . . No. He's like a doctor in a way."

"But a doctor's a man first. And he doesn't deny his nature to become a doctor."

"Nim, there is only one answer to your logic: if a man has to deny his nature to become a priest, he shouldn't be one."

"That makes more sense than some other things you've said. Do you think celibacy makes you a better priest?"

"No, but once I believed it. Once I believed everything the Church taught. Immutable truth, which, it turns out now, is somehow being muted. And I sometimes wonder what will happen if the forms are taken away, one by one."

"They won't need priests any more—just man and God."

McMahon tried to smile. "You make me sound obsolete."

"Do you really believe you have the power to forgive sin?"

"In God's name, yes."

"And so of course you believe in sin."

"Don't you?"

"I don't think I do. Or maybe one sin—dishonesty."

"You just spoke of another," McMahon said, "hurting people."

Nim, moving away from the heater, put her cigarette out

slowly, determinedly. "That's not sin—that's a condition of being human."

"Believe me, so is sin."

She laughed and got up. "Would you like a drink? I bought some Scotch."

"Thank you, I would." McMahon followed her to the kitchen door. "I suppose we ought to eat that pie before . . . soon."

"Before what?"

He caught at the least false excuse available. "I saw a cockroach."

"Only one? They generally come in tandem." She opened the refrigerator door and then closed it again. "Joe, do you want to go to bed with me?"

"Very much."

"Then let's turn out the lights and see what happens."

"I love you very much, Nim. So let's leave the lights on."

"You do sometimes surprise me," she said, going toward him.

19

McMahon washed and washed again his hands in the sacristy before putting on the Mass vestments. Guilt was one thing, but guilt with joy, how manage that? His mouth should be filled with ashes, but it was the taste of apples on his tongue. I will go unto the altar of God: the Mass was the Mass if said by a priest, however guilty the man...to God who gives joy to my youth.

He did not intend to go again to Nim. That had been implicit in their parting. But neither could he yet confess those moments to be sin. God have mercy on us. Christ have mercy on us. God have mercy on us. And in the front pew sat Priscilla Phelan who had never come to weekday Mass before to his knowledge. What angel roused her from her bed, what demon? She kept staring at him as though to read the gospel of hypocrisy whenever he raised his eyes. Poor child of pain, he thought, who comes to steal vengeance from the Lord. What are we at all, frail creatures of flesh pretending spirit, and compensating our grief in the torture of one another? Our father... lead us not into temptation, but deliver us from evil... Tell us what is evil, or silence the voices that accuse.

But Priscilla Phelan had not come to accuse. She waited for him in the courtyard outside the sacristy, and when he came out, she said, "Father, I am sorry for what I said to you on the stoop the other night."

"It was said in anger, and I don't blame you. I tried to help and made a mess of it."

"I made the mess, not telling you the truth in the first place. Now I've done something else, Father."

McMahon drew a deep breath and tried to put down the feeling of nausea rising in his throat.

"I rented the back room to a policeman. Don't ask me why. I guess because I didn't want Dan going any place he'd get in trouble. But now I don't know how to tell him."

"I don't think I can advise you in this, Mrs. Phelan. Except... Dan is sick in several ways, and you can't just set about healing him yourself no matter how much you want to. Let him see Dr. Connelly, and me. I'm not much help, but he talks with me."

"He won't talk to me at all. He keeps watching the door, like I was a policeman too. I made myself come out this morning. I gave him a sleeping tablet. I told him it was a tranquilizer. And I locked the door."

"Then for God's sake go home and unlock it and leave it open. He tried to kill himself. That's the easiest way out for him, don't you see?"

She covered her face with her hands. "What have I done to the man? What have I done to him?"

"It was done long ago, the worst of it—and the rest you've done to one another. With my help."

"Come home with me, Father, I'm afraid."

Down the same street they walked quickly as he had walked with Carlos, but when they reached the Phelan apartment, the man was sleeping like a child. They stood and looked down at him in the bed, the lines in his face all but vanished and a gentle smile on his lips. His wife stood, her arms folded, and out of the corner of his eye, McMahon saw the little cradling motion of her body.

In the living room McMahon said, "Tell him I came and that I'm working on his project. That will give him a kind of peace."

"A kind of peace," she repeated. "And where do I go for mine?"

"I just don't know." He left her sobbing quietly to herself in a corner of the sofa in the darkest part of the room.

During the morning he worked out a letter of inquiry to the Franciscan Brothers which might serve Phelan as a guide in writing one of his own. He tried not to think of Nim, of the hour she would arrive at the precinct headquarters, where she would give her statement and how she would sign it. Nana Marie Lavery, he supposed. He had never even seen her handwriting. He tried not to think of her, but his mind would not stay servant to his will. He was going to have to get out of the city somehow.

He heard the front doorbell ring and Miss Lalor thump down the hall from the kitchen. A couple of minutes later she knocked on the door and handed him a special delivery letter. He dreaded to open it and yet the beat of his heart bade him make haste: the neat handwriting and no return address. Then he saw that it had been postmarked the day before so that it could not be from Nim. He tore open the envelope.

The invitation was engraved. It read:

"You are invited to an exhibition of paintings from the collection of David Wallenstein at Mr. Wallenstein's home, 1090 Fifth Avenue on Monday, the fifth of May, at 4 P.M."

Along with the invitation came the personal card of Everett Wallenstein on the back of which had been written: "Do come. It will be to the interest of our protégée. My father has invited the most important people of the art world." Wallenstein had initialed the note.

And Nim would have gotten the same invitation. McMahon cleared his calendar for four that afternoon.

He saw her the moment he stepped from the bus. She was walking up and down in front of the building; the green suit again, the lovely green suit with the orange scarf at the throat, and the dark hair shining in the sun.

"The fates," she said with a wry smile when he walked up to her. "What is it all about?"

"We'll know soon."

"I was afraid you wouldn't come. I don't think I'd have gone in if you hadn't."

"That's why I came."

"That's why I came too," she said, responding to her own notion of his real reason for coming. "One wants to know—in spite of everything."

People were going into the mansion, not many and mostly men, but people you would identify with painting; at least, knowing of the invitation, you would, McMahon thought.

She gazed out over Central Park for a moment. "You see, Joe, I don't think I believed for a minute that Mr. Wallenstein was really interested in my work."

"In you, yes," McMahon said.

She turned toward the building and they started in. "No. Only in Stu . . . that's what I think now anyway. We'll see."

The old gentleman opened the door to them himself, offering his hand to McMahon. "I am David Wallenstein." He had a cherubic look, the plump pink cheeks that would have rarely needed shaving, mild gray eyes with none of the son's hauteur in them. One could associate him with painting, with collecting, with money, McMahon thought, but not with the making of money. "You are the personal friends Everett invited. I have been curious, I must admit. A priest . . ." Then he looked at Nim. ". . . And a maiden." The sensuous mouth puckered just a little while he gazed at her. He continued to gaze unashamedly even as he suggested that they join the other guests. McMahon had the identical reaction to him he had had to the son, possibly stronger. Where the son had looked at her with an aloof appraisal, the father's eyes grew indulgent, as though by grace of association with young Wallenstein she became a household intimacy.

In the living room beyond the foyer a dozen people had gathered, only two of them women. They stood, highball glasses in hand, in easy camaraderie. When Wallenstein left Nim and McMahon at the door they were accorded the cool glances of nonrecognition.

"I don't like him much," Nim said of the elder Wallenstein.

McMahon did not want to talk of his reaction. "What's yours is mine and what's mine is my own," he murmured.

"Exactly," Nim said.

The walls were hung with the Impressionists which had made the collection famous. It was, someone said, the first time to his knowledge the old boy had opened his doors to the public. He would lend a painting now and then, but never any number of them at a time. Someone else reminded the speaker that the present company could hardly be called the public. Nim and McMahon accepted drinks and went from Monet to Redon. They were waiting as no one else there seemed to be waiting. Two more people arrived, also well known to the others, and then the elder Wallenstein came to the wide doors and spoke from the foyer. "Finish your drinks, gentlemen—and ladies. Then I would ask that you leave your glasses here..."

"The son isn't here," Nim said uneasily.

"Where was it Brogan said yesterday that he'd gone? Drummond Island? You did go to the police this morning, didn't you?"

"Yes. It was mostly about him they questioned me. I think they've made some connection between him and Stu. It could be Drummond Island."

A servant collected the glasses.

Wallenstein raised his hand for attention again. "You will indulge me in a few moments of personal reminiscence. Then we shall look at some more pictures. My son and I have many years of alienation between us, and I am as aware as he is of the feelings of this distinguished group toward his... public image. For much of his apparent superficiality, shall I call it, I am to be blamed. Today I atone. I should have liked myself to be a painter, and from the time Everett was a child I wanted it for him. I surrounded him with the best my fortune could buy—not the worst of the famous but, as you will have observed, the best of the lesser famous as well, most of whom have proven my taste to be as excellent as their own.

"It occurred to me one day when Everett had become

adamant about showing me anything he'd done, that I might have crippled him with such perfectionism. I am rewarded in a way I am not sure I deserved. We were not friends for a long time even though he took his place in the firm. And when he came into his inheritance from his mother, he bought his own house and lived separately—very separately. I was not invited, ever. But one day I invited myself. So much is prologue. Please come with me."

"My God, my God," McMahon said. Nim's fingers were digging into his arm.

They followed the others who followed Wallenstein up the wide hall staircase, the latter among them exchanging whispers of disbelief. They would not easily discard their image of young Wallenstein, the dilettante.

The elder Wallenstein opened the door to a sitting room and threw on the lights. There were perhaps twenty paintings hung in the room. At a glance McMahon would have said they were the work of several artists, the difference in styles, colors and textures, the range from objects to abstraction: but this he and Nim already knew to be likely of the work of Muller-Chase.

"Please, one by one," Wallenstein said, "but this one first."

They gathered round him beneath a nude, the back of a black woman bowed so that her head showed only where the hair tumbled down over her arm, the forlorn shape of an abandoned woman. "This," the old man said, "is what I saw first that day when I presumed to invade his studio."

Nim cleared her throat and pulled McMahon down to where she could whisper to him: "E for ego, self . . . remember?"

Wallenstein then said almost the same thing: "It may seem academic, gentlemen, but Everett insists that E does not stand for his name but for Ego. Perhaps the self which I tried to deny him?"

They went from one group of paintings to another, only three or four in each group. McMahon could not really say whether he liked the nonobjective work or not. The experts were noncommittal, silent.

"He has destroyed hundreds of canvases, preserving only those which tell the truth. His philosophy of art is interesting: he believes an artist is only himself for a little while in any environment. Then he becomes corroded—with praise or blame, with fashion, with what is expected of him by, forgive me, you gentlemen. An artist should preserve only what he achieved at the moment of greatest self-demand, self-recognition. The rest turns him into a barnacle. But perhaps you will listen to him differently from now on, eh, gentlemen?"

Something terrible came into those mild gray eyes again when he said that: greed? arrogance? Power. Maybe that was it, McMahon thought. They were moved along to a painting that McMahon and Nim both recognized. She squeezed his arm. The sketch Broglio had given her would have been the forerunner to this work: the lines of the grocer's back as he stood at the scale were even more poignant in the painting. Wallenstein said of it: "How many generations of heritage went into that, would you say? In Germany a hundred and fifty years ago, my great-grandfather sold coffee by the measure."

"What does it mean?" Nim whispered again. "What does it mean?"

They had come almost full circle of the room to where a silken drapery hung over another frame.

"Everett hung this collection himself in the last week," Wallenstein said. "And yesterday, before he left for Europe, he brought this latest canvas. I have obliged his request that even I not see it until today." He reached up and with the plump, well-manicured hand, drew away the drapery. An envelope was in the corner of the frame, but McMahon saw it only peripherally as the old man took it in his hand. It was the picture that shook both him and Nim so that it seemed like one shudder running through both of them. He put his arm around her and held on tightly.

Realism superimposed on impressionism: the background tone was the smoky amber of the Orthodox church with the suggestion of the brown beams arching, and the pendulous chains shone through the muskiness, the paint seeming not yet dry, but instead of the glass-bowled candles that hung in the church, in the painting hung the severed heads of men. Nim hid her face against McMahon's arm.

He kept staring at the painting, wanting to keep his own balance. The chains seemed to sway a little as though the heads were restless still. The others of the group were reacting now, a murmurous consternation, but the attention shifted to Wallenstein himself. When McMahon looked at him he saw that the cherubic pink of his face had turned to parchment pallor, the hand in which he held the note trembled more and more violently.

A man stepped forward to help him. Wallenstein crumpled the paper and thrust it into the man's hand, and with the same motion pushed the man out of his way, and then the others, his arm stiff before him, and walked from the room with the autonomic step of one who has measured the distance to his collapse.

The man into whose hands he had given the paper uncrumpled it and read what was written, passing it on then to his colleagues. Finally it came to McMahon and Nim.

My dear father: The work you have shown is that of Thomas Stuart Chase, whom I killed with a knife when he agreed that I should perpetrate this hoax. E is for Ego, but Chase's, not mine. Mine I now propose to find in the way he found his. E.

They walked until they found a coffee shop on Madison Avenue, a quiet place, it being well before the dinner hour. They sat opposite each other, not looking directly at one another; or, when their eyes met, it was not in concern or involvement with one another. McMahon leaned an elbow on the table and shaded his eyes with his hand, seeing still in his mind's eye, that last picture, then finally the others. When he looked up Nim was crying.

"What I'm doing, Nim—I'm thinking of the paintings themselves. They're safe. That's the important thing. I almost think it would be the important thing even if the fraud had been successful. I'm wondering if that isn't how Muller himself felt at the end. He could have told me . . ."

She was only half-listening to him, trying to keep from sobbing.

"Why are you crying?"

"Because for the first time in my life I know what it is I'm hating and it feels good."

"To hate—or to cry?"

"Both."

"What are you hating, Nim?"

"That man—from the first minute I saw him. The arrogance—no, the voraciousness—that's it. It's what I ran away from, Joe, that soft, mine-all-mine possessiveness. The smugness, smothering . . . God, how I hate it, him."

"I see. You've got a lot of things mixed up, Nim."

"Maybe I do. He's like my mother, and in a crazy way, his son is like my father—you know—Wall Street—a physicist making Dow chemicals to please her. You're right. I am mixed up."

"Why can't you just think about the paintings?"

"Because they're there! In his house."

"You'd think it was he who killed your friend, and it wasn't."

"But it was. He'd kill all of us. He's Hitler, Joe, the way Stu told it to Mr. Rosenberg. And if Stu could see his pictures hanging there, he'd go in and destroy them."

"But he'd be wrong, Nim. And I don't think he would. Or the paintings wouldn't be there now. The devil has many disguises, but the Christ in us knows them every one. It's an old saw, but the devil quotes scripture. Hitler might have liked Mozart. But Mozart was still Mozart. All I'm saying, Nim—love the pictures. Love what you *can* love, even if you can't love what you want to love. That's where the mix-up is, I think."

Nim leaned her head back in the booth while the waitress

served their coffee. When the girl had gone, she said: "I'm beginning to get things sorted out. I'm trying to protect something. What?"

"A couple of things," McMahon hedged.

"Me. I'm protecting me. I wanted him—I wanted his child—you—the pictures—I wanted to protect them. But as you say, they are protected. It's all right now, Joe. As long as I know what's going on in me. It's when I don't know. That's when I'm in trouble." She blew her nose. "Will you go to the police?"

"Someone there will." He realized and said: "I have the note in my pocket. I didn't know what to do with it. I want to think some things out first. I don't like to think about young Wallenstein either, but I'm going to. I don't like what I remember of him, the way he looked at you that first time in his house. He wanted everything too."

"Not me," Nim said. "He didn't want me. What he wanted was to see if I had anything of Stu's."

"When I think of the coldness," McMahon went on, following his own train of thought, "with which he looked at the face of the man in the morgue and then came out and talked to me about you—that dinner he gave us—the tears in your house: what did they mean, Nim?"

"He said it: they were for himself. Like mine just now. Not remorse, not grief, not even anger. He'd have seen Stu in that painting of mine and he'd have known of himself that he wasn't even as good as me. Remember? At the door he asked how my father felt about my painting now."

McMahon thought about it. "I wonder if that was the moment when he decided on this note that's in my pocket. Vengeance over all."

"Uber alles," Nim said. "He would have loved Stu once I think, wherever they met, however often. But it would have been a kind of hell for him to keep those paintings when he couldn't make his own. And that father to run away from."

"Maybe that's it and now he thinks he's free. Sometimes I've thought that Muller didn't live to finish what he was trying to say at the end, I took the knife away from him. Maybe if he'd finished it, he'd have said: and given him a brush."

"Maybe, maybe, maybe. It's all over as far as I'm concerned. I'll be able to think of the paintings now. Stu is dead, and here I am with you, ready for another kind of dying."

"I'm going away for a few days," McMahon said. "Some place cheap by the sea where there aren't any people this time of year." He looked up at her suddenly. He had not meant to, but he did.

Her eyes were waiting for his, expecting them, the question in them. She shook her head.

20

When he got back to the rectory there was a message for him: Phelan had been picked up again by the police. He went at once to the station house.

Priscilla Phelan was pleading with the officer at the charge desk to be allowed to see her husband. She was on the raw edge of profanity. McMahon knew too well her mercurial temper. He called out her name. She ran to meet him.

"He'll be all right," McMahon said. "Tell me what happened."

"He went for a walk and that bastard in the backroom followed him."

"Where?"

"To the building where Muller was killed."

"It was not far," McMahon said, as though that were the important thing. He asked the desk officer to phone and see if he might go up to the interrogation room. Permission was granted. "I'll come back as soon as I can," he told Mrs. Phelan. "Just sit down quietly and don't make any trouble."

"Stay with him, Father. Don't leave him alone with them."

The point on which they were interrogating Phelan when McMahon entered the room was where he had met Everett Wallenstein. Phelan, slumped in the straight chair, circled in light, denied having ever met the man at all. While Brogan questioned, Traynor strolled over to meet the priest. "Counselor," he said.

McMahon said, "You know that Wallenstein left a confession to the murder?"

Traynor nodded.

Brogan, aware then of the priest, said, "Just tell us what you were doing in that building today, Dan."

"I wanted to see something upstairs. That's all."

"The poor devil could hardly climb the stairs," Brogan said to McMahon, "but he still won't tell us what he was looking for. His fingerprints were all over that goddamned cot we found up there."

McMahon said, "The painting, Dan? Is that it? The severed heads?"

Phelan looked in his direction, trying to see through the wall of light.

"Let's sit and talk without all that light. Let's try it that way, lieutenant."

So, with the priest's help, Phelan told of how he had first followed Muller, and then discovered the painting he was working on at the top of the abandoned building. "I'd go there sometimes when I knew he wasn't there and just sit on the cot, just to be there."

"Sexual fantasies, Dan?"

Phelan nodded. "But religious too, Father. I got them all mixed up."

McMahon said to the detectives, "This is Dr. Connelly's work, not ours." Then to Phelan: "Dan, were you in the building when he was killed?"

"I'd been there most of the night. That's where I went when I left Priscilla. It's where I was before too. But when I heard the voices in the basement, you could hear them up the stairwell, I got out as fast as I could. I didn't want him to find me. I swear to God I didn't know what was going on. I didn't know. And later when I found out what happened, I just kept away."

"But why the hell didn't you go home?" Brogan said.

"Because that's where my wife was," Phelan shouted hoarsely.

"Okay," Traynor said. "He's in no shape to do any more talking now. You can take him home, Father." He got up from the table around which the four of them had been sitting.

Brogan said, "To think you brought Wallenstein in to us, Father, and I let him go. Drummond Island—and all the time he was skipping the country."

"Where's Drummond Island?"

"It's away out off the coast of Maine. His old man owns it."

McMahon gave Traynor the crumpled note.

When the police were gone he sat down again with Phelan.

"I'd like to go to confession, Father." He looked around the small, bare room with its smoke-grayed walls. "I don't think I can make it to the church."

"It's a long ways in your condition," McMahon said.

Phelan closed his eyes for a moment. "It's funny, you saying that, Father. I was thinking this morning of my own father, a tough brute of an Irishman. He was always trying to squeeze a dollar out of my mother, and she'd say, 'It's a long ways to payday, lover.' Always lover. And he'd say, 'It'll be a longer one, Tess, if you don't give me the dollar now.' Why do the Irish drink so much, Father?"

"I'm not sure they all do," McMahon said, "but I drink too much myself."

"Why?"

"It's a long ways to payday."

Phelan managed a crack of a smile. "I can't get over that family in the hospital with me. Love, it's the only word for it."

"They're real," McMahon said.

"Oh, yes. They know what it's about. No dark corners. You know, they'd kill for one another, Father. They wouldn't say it was right. But they'd say it was love."

McMahon drew a long breath. "Dan, I want to tell you something that's on my conscience: I was with Detective Brogan in the bar on Eighth Street when they picked you up. I'd gone out for a few drinks with him. I didn't know why we'd wound up in that particular spot until I saw you. You were informed on by a priest, Dan."

"I wasn't running away. Just staying away—in a place I felt comfortable."

"I know."

After a minute Phelan said: "It's all so rotten, so crooked, getting sex out of pictures."

"Dan, it's a very common thing. Dr. Connelly will tell you that. That's why I want you to keep seeing him."

"He can't change me."

"He can help you live with yourself—whether it's with Priscilla or not."

"Does it come with a guarantee?"

"No. Only confession comes with a guarantee. And even that is on your own bond."

"'Nothing is given to man': I like that song."

"He's given some choices if he's got the guts to make them."

Phelan put his hand to his breast, to where the knife wound was scarcely healed. "I chose—and I couldn't even do that right."

"I've written a draft letter that might be some help to you. I'd suggest you write the Franciscan Brothers if it turns out that's still what you want when you get things straightened out."

Phelan gave a dry little laugh. "It was a dream—lying in the nice white sheets of the hospital. I should've done it long ago if I was going to. I'm not going to give the Lord back this rotten lump of clay."

"He made it, Dan, and he'd have known what was going to happen to it—even as you and I don't know now. Do you remember the story of St. Ignatius? A soldier, a dissolute man in the days when even the pope was corrupt."

"I don't feel corrupt. I say it, but I don't feel it. Another sin?"

"You are the judge of that."

"The new church again. I want the old one!"

"Then I'm not your priest, Dan," McMahon said quietly.

"Take me home," Phelan said. "I don't think I could find it on my own."

"Home is in you. And you've got to find it yourself."

"All right, all right, Father. She'll be waiting for me, and maybe that's all right—if we can stand the dark corners."

"Dear man," McMahon said, "you are not the only one with the dark corners. They're in every mortal one of us. Which is strange, if in the beginning—if there was a beginning and God said it . . . Let there be light."

Phelan looked at him. "You don't want to hear my confession, do you, Father?"

"No, I don't, but I will if you want it."

Phelan shook his head and lifted himself carefully from the chair. "Let's go."

21

McMahon, with police permission to visit it, left the next day for Drummond Island. The Coast Guard ferried him and the local police officers out. The caretaker, a part-time lobsterman, agreed to put McMahon up for a few days in his own cottage. After they had sealed and padlocked the big house, the police returned to the mainland.

There were no long beaches on which to run, only sandy coves when the tide was out, sheltered half-around by cliffs where the scrub pine was bent by the gales of centuries. But there was the sea and the sky and the stillness except for the gulls and the wind and the wash of the waves which were in themselves a kind of stillness. And the sun on his naked body. It ought all to have healed him, but it only salted the wound. He saw Nim everywhere. Sometimes he would look for an instant into the sun, and the afterglow against his eyelids became a golden cross, then the monstrance at the moment of elevation. To him now sign without substance, ceremony without worship, man without God.

He walked miles around the island, groping through the tangle of fallen timber and new growth, toward and away from the sea. The wild flowers of spring, violets and Mayflowers, and those with names he had forgotten bloomed toward the sun, and jack-in-the-pulpits came out in the shade. Jack-in-the-pulpits: the name went round and round in his head. One night before the fire after the lobsterman had gone to bed, he got up and took an old encyclopedia down from among the musty books. "Jack-in-the-pulpit: . . . the part that looks like the preacher is the slender stalk . . .

enclosed in a leaflike growth which resembles the pulpit . . . a sounding board that extends behind and over . . . The plant grows from a root filled with a burning juice . . ." My God, my God, why hast thou forsaken me? But you've got it wrong, Joseph. My son, my son . . .

And from here Muller-Chase, loaned this refuge by his friend, young Wallenstein, had fled, according to the lobsterman. "He couldn't take it somehow. He'd pick up a tangle of seaweed from the shore and say, 'This is more like it, the slime of the earth and the sea, and the little faces looking out, making mouths for help.' And you know, neighbor, I'd look and I'd see those faces, just for the minute, mind you. But I understood him and I knew why he always had to go back to the city. It was lonesome when he went, but I said to myself, I'd be more lonesome where he's going."

McMahon knew that for all his longing for the sea and the shore, for the salt air and the birds flying, forever flying, he too had to go back to the city, to the little faces looking out of windows and making mouths for help. On the plane back a week later he decided he would see Nim once more and tell her about the island and the lobsterman. And then he knew it would be better to write to her. And finally he knew that silence would be the best of all.

The monsignor embraced him, and Miss Lalor put on her hat and went out to buy a steak. Purdy and Gonzales between them bought a bottle of wine for dinner, and Purdy, on the monsignor's instructions, took it from the slanting shelf of the liquor store and carried it home like a baby. All this they laughed at at the table, and Miss Lalor grew as red in the face as the monsignor. She had had but a sip of the wine. One of the Irish who did not drink, McMahon thought, and he wondered about Phelan.

After dinner, while the other priests went about the parish work, the monsignor and McMahon went into the study. The old man brought out a bottle of cognac. "Napoleon,

Joseph. I've had it since Christmas. You look fine—as brown as one of themselves. Did you spend all the money?"

"Most of it on the fare," McMahon said.

"Good!"

"But I saved the ten dollars I owed you."

"Keep it till payday. You'll want plenty of work now, Joseph. You'll need it, hard work that will tire you out. I've got it for you. I'm not giving up on remodeling the school myself. I was thinking of a bazaar in the summer maybe . . ."

McMahon sipped the cognac.

"No toast, Joseph?"

"To peace," McMahon said. He could think of no other.

"Exactly. It'll come to you after a while. I know from experience. You wouldn't think it to look at me now. But the good Lord knows there's times he has to wait on the frailty of man. Sure, it's all he has to make priests out of, mere men. And he needs them."

"Why?"

"The people need them and he needs the people or there'd be none of us on earth at all."

"We need one another," McMahon said. "That's all."

"That's the way you feel now. When you've started your penance and with your morning mass you'll feel different. You weren't asked to say Mass while . . . you were away?"

"No."

"Good."

"I was alone on an island, Monsignor—except for a lobsterman." He looked the old man straight in the face. He saw the change in expression, the little shadow of doubt in what he had believed of McMahon. Or was it that he doubted McMahon was telling the truth now?

It was the latter, for the old man said, "Well, I'm glad you're back."

"No scandal," McMahon said with deliberate provocation.

Again the old man was not sure. "What do you mean, Joseph?"

"I gave no scandal."

"You don't have to say it out to me." The old man, reassured, poured himself a drop more brandy and was about to add to McMahon's.

McMahon covered his glass.

"Why won't you drink, Joseph?"

McMahon pushed the glass a little farther from him on the table. "You know, Monsignor, it has just occurred to me, I may never drink again."

"It's better than some things. A priest needs a drop now and then."

McMahon could feel the crawling urge to move in his neck, in his spine. "I think I'll go into the church for a few minutes, Monsignor, if you'll forgive me."

"Go, by all means. As the kids say nowadays, that's where it is. I'm beginning to catch up. But at my age, Joseph, you never catch up. You just step aside. I'll be doing that soon. I'd do it now—if I knew who was taking my place. I suppose they're right, not letting us know or having a say in the matter. There's an instinct in all of us—father and son. Go. I wish you felt like talking. I've missed our talks, but I was missing them before you went away, a long time before, even before that artist's death and that girl. There, I've said it. It's out in the open and we'll both feel the better for it. Go. The Lord's waiting, and I'm waiting on the Lord."

McMahon got as far as the sacristy door, but he did not go into the church. He took the subway downtown and walked through the West Village to the East Village on Eighth Street, then down to Fifth. Though he got no answer when he rang Nim's bell, he went up the stairs where the light was as frail as that in Mrs. Phelan's tenement. He knew, reaching the top floor, that she was gone, goods, pictures and all, for in the corner outside her door was the one piece of furniture she could not take with her, the piano.

He stood and looked at it for a long time, and then out the window to the Orthodox church, its simple façade with its complex cross, in the great hulking shadow of the old school building, and he began in his mind to compose a letter: "I will find you, Nim, so you may as well help me. There will be a place. I can teach music, you know..."

"ELEANOR THE PRIVATE EYE IS UTTERLY ENDEARING!"
The New York Times Book Review

Join Eleanor Roosevelt—

in the White House as the First Lady tries to find a murderer...

at Hyde Park—where financial fraud became murder most foul...

as she puts on her investigative cap in two scandalous cases by

ELLIOT ROOSEVELT

MURDER AND THE FIRST LADY
69937-0/$2.95US/$3.95Can

THE HYDE PARK MURDER
70058-1/$2.95US/$3.95Can

"Delightful! Elliot Roosevelt brings his father and mother to life. Agatha Christie's Miss Marple couldn't have done a better job than Eleanor Roosevelt."
John Barkham Reviews